Summer Nights

—Montana Beach—
Book 3

D. Allen

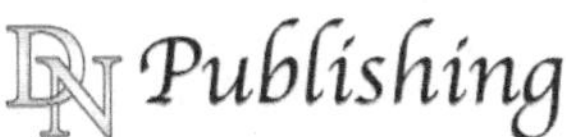

DN Publishing

Summer Nights
Montana Beach, Book 3

www.DavidNethBooks.com

ISBN: 978-1-963602-00-5

Subscribe to the author's newsletter for updates and exclusive content:
DavidNethBooks.com/Newsletter

Follow the author at:
www.facebook.com/DavidNethBooks

Also by D. Allen

Montana Beach
Summer Stay

Summer Job

Summer Nights

Small Town Christmas
A Christmas Reunion

A Christmas Charade

A Christmas Spark

A Christmas Song

A Christmas Departure

A Christmas Wedding

A Christmas Escape

A Christmas Renovation

Standalone
Snow After Christmas

Chapter One:
ADRIAN

It's nearly four in the morning, but the digital clock on the nightstand has my full attention. I watch as the blinking light counts each passing second, wondering how long I'll get to lay here with Malcolm before he gets the phone call.

I pray that it doesn't come. Every night I pray, but his phone inevitably rings. Even though I'm still wrapped in his arms, I can't help but think about him leaving.

I suck in a shuddering breath and close my eyes. Maybe tonight my prayers will be answered and we'll wake up in the morning together. This is the latest he's stayed in a while. Usually he's out the door shortly after we finish, which makes it nearly impossible to get to sleep.

Summer Nights

That's the worst part about loving him. The loneliness that follows his exit. He always tries to move quietly, telling me to go back to sleep when I get up to walk him out, but it's no use. I'm always left feeling empty. Alone. Sad.

I focus on his steady breaths, letting it soothe me so I can fall asleep, but the sudden burst of his ringtone makes me jump. Malcolm stirs. He pulls away from me and reaches for his phone on the opposite nightstand.

I know the drill. Stay silent and still. He's never come right out and told me to, but it's kind of obvious that he wants privacy since he leaves the room every time it's a phone call.

"Hello?" He says once he's at the door.

I close my eyes and pretend that the call never came. That he's still lying beside me. But his voice carries from the living room and I know this is really happening.

"I was tired, so I pulled over to take a nap."

I stare at the clock again, watching more seconds pass by.

"I'm about forty minutes out," he says.

It's quiet. My heart races in fear that I was heard somehow.

"No, just tired," he finally says. "Like I just said. Go back to sleep. I'll be home soon."

I close my eyes and try to think of something else

to ease the heartache. I know what's coming.

"Love you, too."

It's like a physical pain in my chest.

Malcolm comes back in when he's off the phone and shakes me gently. "Hey, I have to get going."

"Yeah, I heard," I mutter. I keep my eyes on the clock. 3:52. That has to be a record.

"I'm sorry, babe, but I have to keep up appearances." He rubs my arm. "At least for a little while longer."

"I know."

He pauses, then asks, "Remember what I promised you?"

I don't say anything. It almost seems like it'll never happen at this point.

"Hey." He nudges me until I roll over to look up at him. "Someday soon it'll just be me and you. *You're* the one I want to be with. I love you."

Hearing him say it helps make me feel a little better. "I love you, too."

He kisses my forehead and then disappears into the bathroom.

Despite my best efforts, I retreat to my negative thoughts. I love him and he says he loves me, but a part of me also thinks that if he truly loved me that this would be an easy choice for him.

I'm always wrestling with myself, wondering if I'm a bad person or just a man in love. I'm not the one deciding to betray a commitment. I've made my commitment. To him.

Malcolm's the one who's married.

But I know he can't just leave her. As Malcolm's pointed out before, I'm quite a bit younger than him, which means he has more history with his wife than I've ever had with anybody. Leaving her isn't just leaving a woman he's no longer in love with, but also leaving his home and disrupting his whole life.

And coming out.

Nobody knows that he's gay…or at least likes men. I don't really know *what* he is, just that he's not completely straight. That alone would change his life a lot more than a divorce would. Especially if his wife found out about me. He could be robbed of everything in divorce court. I don't want to see his life ruined, even if it means he has to stay married to her a little bit longer.

Of course, if she decides to leave him, things might be easier for him. He could move here to Montana Beach with me. My little house would be fine for the two of us.

Malcolm comes out of the bathroom and finishes pulling on his clothes. "Go back to sleep," he whispers. "The sun's going to be up soon and you'll need your rest for work tomorrow night."

I sit up in bed.

"What?" he asks.

I wave him forward. He leans down and kisses me and I pull him back on the bed with me, laughing. He pushes at my shoulders, pinning me against the mattress, and kisses me the way I like. The way that usually leads to—

He pulls away. "I need to get going."

"Why don't you stay?" I kneel on the bed, hoping that it's enticing enough for him to crawl in again and pretend that she never called.

"I can't stay. You know that."

"Just tell her you fell back asleep."

He gives me a look. "She's smarter than that."

"We can pretend that you've already left your wife. Imagine sleeping straight through until morning, wrapped in each other. Then, before you get up, I'll bring you breakfast in bed."

"Oh yeah?" He smirks.

"Yeah. We can lay around and watch TV all day— or anything else you want." I reach for his hand and slowly work my fingers between his. "Please, baby? Won't you stay?"

Malcolm squeezes our interlocked hands before pulling away. "That sounds really nice, but not tonight. Maybe if she goes out of town." He steps out of the room and I follow. By the front door, he grabs his boots and pulls them on.

"Don't you want to stay? Don't you want to be with me? Don't you want to not have to say goodbye at four in the morning? Don't you wish that we could be together all the time? Don't you miss me?" I suck in a shuddering breath. Thankfully, it's still dark.

He cups my face in his hands. "Of course I miss you. All the time."

"Then stay. Please?"

Leaning forward, he kisses me again. "I wish it were that simple."

"Then make it simple!" Anger. That's what'll save me from having him see me cry.

"Babe, I can't."

I cross my arms and refuse to look at him. He doesn't move, so at least I have his attention.

"When are you going to finally divorce her?" I ask in a small voice.

"When the time's right."

"When will that be?"

"I don't know."

"I need to know."

"It doesn't matter what I say," he says. "Even if I said I was going home to tell her right now, I'd still be leaving. I can't stay here tonight. I'm sorry."

He's right. I know that. I'm being selfish. I just hate having to share him. It's getting old. Why should she be allowed to have his mornings, his birthdays, his holidays? When will I have more than just a few of his nights? I'm starting to think that day will never come.

I feel him step toward me and wrap his arms around me, pulling me in for a tight hug. He kisses me again and then moves to the door.

"Get some sleep," he says. "I'll text you in the morning. I love you."

"I love you, too."

He gives me one last lingering look and then disappears out the door.

Almost immediately, it feels like a physical pressure is pushing on my chest, making it hard to breathe. I never thought I'd be so committed to someone that I don't feel complete when they're not around, but that's exactly what I'm feeling. Empty.

I shuffle back to my bedroom and lay down. The bed feels huge without him, but I keep to my side anyway, hoping that by some miracle, this will all be a dream in the morning.

I wish I could just sleep away the hours until we're together again, but I know I can't. I have to work tomorrow. And it's not like I can just *not* go in. I own the bar.

Summer Nights

How did it get to this? I'm a business owner. I'm a homeowner. I have great friends. I'm healthy. From the outside, it seems like I have it all together. So then why do I feel so messed up?

I try to think about the positives. It's not like Malcolm has changed his mind about leaving his wife. He just isn't ready yet. I can't push him to do that if he hasn't gotten to that point. He needs to do it on his own terms, otherwise he'll always be looking over his shoulder. I just need to have patience.

Soon enough he'll be all mine and no one else's. We'll wake up together and go to bed together. He'll rush home to see me instead of having to watch the time while he's with me. Maybe we'll even get a dog. We can walk it together after dinner. People will tell us how happy they are that we're happy. We'll have the rest of our lives to grow old together. Malcolm may have a head-start on me, but when I'm his age, our twenty-year age gap won't be a big deal. Especially since we'll have each other.

When he leaves his wife, things will be much better.

Things will be perfect.

He'll be mine.

Chapter Two:
TYLER

"Morning Mom." I lean down and kiss my mother on the cheek shortly after I wake up. She's propped up in her hospital bed in the living room.

"Morning, dear," she says. "Did you sleep all right?"

"Mm-hmm." I nod. "Do you need anything?"

"No thanks. Your sister's been taking care of everything. Did you get yourself some breakfast?"

"Not yet."

"Well, go and get something to eat. I don't need you shriveling up on me."

I smile and squeeze her hand once before stepping into the small kitchen.

Summer Nights

Mom is in the final stages of breast cancer. She's had a double mastectomy, but the cancer continues to spread throughout her body. The doctors say there's nothing left for them to do except heavy radiation, which my mother is adamantly against. At this point, unfortunately, it's a matter of keeping her comfortable until the end.

"Oh good, you're up," Bailey says when I saunter into the kitchen. She's putting away the dishes from the rack beside the sink. "Mom's had breakfast, her meds, and is watching TV."

I nod. "Yeah, I just talked to her."

"Would you mind helping her clean up before you leave tonight?" She dries a plate and sets it in the cupboard. "I have plans with some of my friends after work and by the time I get back it'll be about time for Mom to go to bed."

Working until after two in the morning *and* having to be up the next morning to help with Mom is tiring to say the least. Luckily, I don't have to be up super early. Bailey usually handles things before she has to go to work at eleven. So if I wake up by ten, that still gives me about seven hours of sleep a night. It's doable.

"Am I making her dinner, too?" I cross the tiny kitchen and pull out a box of cereal from the cupboard.

Bailey hands me a bowl from the rack. "If you don't

mind. I gave her some of the leftovers in the fridge last night."

"That's fine, but who's going to be here when *I* go to work?" I grab the milk from the fridge. The door bangs against the edge of the table that's squeezed in the corner and blocks Bailey in by the sink. We have no dining room and no space in the living room now that Mom's hospital bed is set up in there, so the kitchen's the only place the table can go.

"I'll make sure I'm home by eight."

"I start work at seven." I take a seat at the table and fill the bowl.

Bailey looks back into the living room where Mom is propped up in her hospital bed. "An hour alone can't hurt, can it?"

"Maybe not, but it could also be the most crucial hour of her life."

"You're being dramatic."

I point the spoon at her and some milk drips onto the table. "I'm being safe." I wipe away the mess.

She sighs. "I'll call Megan next door and see if she can sit and watch TV with her."

"That would work. Is she the nurse?"

"Yeah, but I don't know how thrilled she's going to be with the idea of taking on another charge after her shift ends," she says.

"It's only an hour and we can give her a little something."

My sister hooks and eyebrow and looks up at me. "You better be making good tips tonight because I don't have the money to pay her."

I finish chewing as I consider that. "Yeah, that should be fine. Sometime I want to sit down with you so we can figure out the bills. I want to have everything in order for when—"

"Sure, I'll have to double check my schedule at work."

Bailey doesn't like talking about Mom's approaching death. She doesn't have long. I'm trying to treat it as business so that I'm not completely devastated when she goes.

Trying. It's easier said than done.

After Bailey heads off to work, I help Mom get washed up. She tries to do most of it herself—knowing that her children don't want to be the ones to bathe her—but she gets tired easily, so I have to take over.

Soon enough, she's clean, changed into a fresh set of PJ's, and sitting up in her bed with a book.

"Stop fussing over me," she says after the third time I've peeked my head in to check on her. I've already used the vacuum and scoured the room for dirty dishes. I've run out of excuses. "Do something for yourself. I'll be fine for a little bit."

"Are you sure?" I ask.

"Yes! Go out and enjoy the day while you still can. You're always such a night owl. You need to see the sun once in a while! It's good for you."

I know Mom will probably be fine for half an hour while I go for a run, but after telling Bailey this morning that she shouldn't leave her alone for an hour, I know I'd be a hypocrite if I did the same.

So I call Mrs. Heaton from across the street to come over and have lunch with my mom. She's not exactly my mom's best friend, but at least they're friendly with each other. In such a small town, too, everyone knows that my mom's not doing so well. Most people are usually happy to help out.

By time I get out in the sunshine and start running—stretching my legs and making my heart rate jump—the sun is beating down hard on Montana Beach. I don't know if it's the run, the sun, or a combination of both, but I do feel better as I run up and down the streets in town. Guess Mom was right.

The more my feet hit the pavement, the more I can feel my worries about Mom, money, and everything else slip away from me. This is just what I needed to clear my head and keep me going for another day. It's why I try to run several times a week. Especially now that Mom doesn't have much longer left.

I spot Adrian out at his mailbox when I slow to a walk on my way back. He lives right next door. I tug the headphones out of my ears and wave at him as I try to catch my breath. I'm dripping with sweat and lift up the bottom of my shirt to my forehead to wipe it away.

"Morning," he says.

"Morning? It's like twelve-thirty."

"Oh," he says with a yawn. "It took me a while to get to sleep last night."

I raise my eyebrows and grin. "Oh? That kind of a night?"

He tries to act surprised. "What are you talking about?"

"I saw an extra car in your driveway last night. Is that the same man-friend you've been so secretive about?" It's been kind of obvious that he's seeing someone. He's always in a rush to close up the bar each night, always texting, usually smiling when he checks his phone. I actually kind of miss him because of it.

Adrian smirks. "Maybe."

"I take it you had a good night then?"

He looks away. "Uh, yeah, it was great. I love seeing him."

"So when are the rest of us going to get to meet him?"

He scrunches his eyebrows. "The rest of us?"

"Me, Jessie, and Robyn. The whole crew."

"Oh. I don't know. He's not out yet."

"Do we know him?" I ask.

He shakes his head. "No, he's from North Beach."

"So what's the big deal?"

"I just don't want to, okay!" he snaps.

"Easy, Adrian, I'm only kidding."

He exhales. "Sorry. I just don't feel comfortable introducing him as my boyfriend if he's still—if he hasn't come out yet."

I nod. "I guess that makes sense. Is he going to come out soon?"

"I don't know." He's annoyed now.

"Oh. Well, I'd still like to meet him sometime. I'm sure the girls would, too. Do they know about him?"

"I'm not sure." He turns toward his house and then turns back to me. "Look, I didn't sleep well last night and I'd love to sneak in another hour before I have to go to work. I'll see you tonight?"

"Of course."

He smacks my arm lightly and turns away. "Sounds good, I'll see you then!"

Summer Nights

"Can you make sure the fridge under the bar is all stocked up?" Adrian asks at the Nine that night.

It's the bar he owns on First Street in town and is basically the only center of nightlife in town if you don't count the dive bar a few doors down.

"Sure thing." I carry a rack of clean glasses from the kitchen to the bar and set them down.

Adrian sits at the bar and scribbles in a notepad, making up the drink specials for tonight, like he does every night.

I put half of the glasses in the cooler so they're cold and the other half on the shelf. The wine glasses slide conveniently onto a rack behind the bar.

"Anything good for tonight?" I ask.

"Uh, just trying to rotate stuff that hasn't been selling a lot lately," he replies. "Trying to bring up sales on everything, you know?"

"Yeah."

"Do you know how much of that new stuff we have left?"

I narrow my eyes. "What new stuff?"

"The beer. It's got like a red label on it or something…" His voice trails off.

I shrug. "I got nothing."

"Never mind, I'll go check myself." He slides off the stool and walks to the stock room.

Something's bothering him. I'm kind of worried that he's going through a rough time and not talking to anyone about it. I wonder if it has to do with his boyfriend. I know that if I bring it up, he'll tell me that with everything *I'm* going through, I shouldn't be worrying about him, but I am.

I've actually been thinking about him a lot now that I work with him. It's a fairly new arrangement, but it seems to be working. We haven't had any major disagreements. He offered me the job because he knew that I could use the money. Plus, I'm sure he thought it'd be fun to work with his friend. That was one of the main reasons why I took it, actually.

Okay, the money was good too.

"Yeah, we have plenty," he says when he returns. "Looks like that's our special for tonight. It's new and nobody knows about it. Dropping the price a bit should get people to try it."

"Do you want me to write the specials on the board?"

He gives me a look. "Not a chance. I saw the crap you tried to pull off when you first started."

"It was a masterpiece!" I joke.

"It was crap." He laughs. "No, I'll take care of it. What you can do is mop the floors so they have time to dry before we open up."

"Yes, sir!"

"That's what I like to hear!" he calls to me as I head toward the cleaning closet in the back.

Working at the Nine is such a relaxed atmosphere and the fact that I get to work with Adrian makes it even better. We have a lot of fun. Usually we'll walk to and from work together. He's a big reason why I've been able to stay sane with everything going on with my mom. He's my best friend.

I go to the office and find Adrian clicking around on the computer after closing. "Tables are wiped, the kitchen floors are mopped, the dishes are done, and the bar is all stocked. Is there anything else you want done?"

He turns off the computer and snatches his keys from the hook. "No, that should be it. Is Frankie ready?"

"He said he was almost done."

"Okay good. Because I'm ready to go." He hits the lights and hurries over to the kitchen, nearly getting smacked in the face when Frankie emerges through the swinging door.

"All done, boss." He notices Adrian's surprise and adds, "Sorry, did I get you?"

"Just barely missed. But that's awesome, thanks for doing that," Adrian says. "I'll see you tomorrow."

"Night guys!"

I unlock the door so Frankie can leave and wait by it for Adrian to finish shutting off all the lights.

"Floors, drinks, deposit, lights…I think that's everything," he mutters to himself. "Are you ready?"

"Just waiting on you."

"Thanks."

We step outside and Adrian locks the door behind us.

"You seem to be in a rush again tonight," I say as we walk down the sidewalk. "What are you so anxious for?"

Adrian turns and smiles at me.

"Ah."

"Yeah. He works during the day and I obviously work a weird shift, so this is about the only time we get to see each other."

"Right." I don't know what it is, but at this moment, I don't want to hear about Adrian's boyfriend. We usually spend our walks home talking and joking about anything and everything — you know, being *friends*. But with Adrian's head buried in his phone tonight, I might as well be walking home by myself.

I try to push it away as irrational. He's dating

someone. He's usually on his phone anyway. He has less time for friends. It's just the way things work. I need to grow up and get over it.

"Do you mind if tomorrow—"

Adrian stops where he is, which makes me stop too.

"What are you doing?" I ask.

He stares at his phone and doesn't respond at first. When he looks up he breathes a heavy sigh. "He's not coming."

Chapter Three:
ADRIAN

"Who's not coming?" Tyler asks. "Your boyfriend?"

"He's not—" Whether or not Malcolm is technically my boyfriend is not something I want to discuss right now. What do you call the person you're sleeping with who is still married to someone else? It's complicated. "Malcolm's not coming." I wave my phone up with the text conversation still up.

"Oh." There's a moment of quiet before Tyler adds, "Why don't you try calling him instead of texting? Maybe you can convince him to come?"

I shake my head. "No, I'm not going to call him." That would really mess things up if his wife sees it. Besides, am I really that desperate for his attention that

I need to beg him to come see me? The overwhelming sense of loneliness that hit me the moment I read his text is more than likely a sign that I *am* that desperate. I'm tired of feeling like this.

"You should let him know you're disappointed at least," Tyler says.

"Yeah." I hit reply and write, *When can I see you again?*

We keep walking, both of us quiet in the late-night darkness.

My phone dings again with another message.

Not sure yet. We got in a huge fight about how I haven't been home much. I have to stick around until the dust settles.

I let out a heavy sigh. "Great."

"What is it?" Tyler asks.

I type back, *We don't have to live this way, you know,* and slip my phone in my back pocket. "He doesn't know when he's going to be free again."

"That sucks."

"Yeah."

My phone dings again.

Sorry :(

I ignore it. If he was really sorry he'd be here.

When we get to our houses, Tyler grabs my arm to stop me from going to mine.

"Did you want to hang out tonight?" he asks. "I

know it isn't the same as being with your—being with Malcolm, but at least you won't be alone."

It's sweet that Tyler's trying to help out, but I don't know how he'll be able to help. He's not Malcolm.

I shake my head. "No, I can't ask you to do that." I glance at my phone and see it's almost three in the morning. "It's late. You're probably tired. I don't want to bother you."

"No really, it's no bother. I'd actually really like it. It's been a while since we've hung out outside of work. And it's not like I'll have a far walk to get home."

I shrug. "That's true."

"Come on." He starts leading me to my house with extra vigor. "We can watch a movie or something."

My house is dark, but I only turn on the TV to let it illuminate the living room.

"Pick something, I'll be back in a minute," I tell him before disappearing into my room.

I change out of my jeans and into a pair of gym shorts and a tank top. I grab my phone and check for anymore messages from Malcolm.

Nothing.

I shouldn't be surprised and I shouldn't even be mad. He has a wife who rightfully wants to see him. I just wish he would tell her how he feels so he doesn't have to keep splitting his time. My finger hovers over the call button, but I ultimately slip my phone in my pocket.

Snatching the blanket from my bed, I come out into the living room with it wrapped around me.

"Find anything?" I take a seat on the opposite end of the couch and splay out the blanket between us.

"Something scary or something funny?" he asks.

"Funny. Definitely funny." I don't need another reason to be upset tonight.

He clicks over on one of the comedies I have queued up on my Netflix account and we both get settled in on the couch. I feel his feet sneak under the blanket and I squeeze mine between his leg and the couch cushion.

"Is that going to bother you?" I ask.

He shakes his head. "No, that's fine."

Although the movie plays, I'm too preoccupied with Malcolm. I wish he was here. At least I have Tyler's company. He's a good friend. My best friend, really. I usually group the girls in with my best friends as well, but Tyler and I see each other almost every day. Our lives are a lot more interconnected than with the girls.

But I still miss Malcolm. The worst part is that I don't know when I'll see him again. When I'll hold him. When we'll actually start to put into motion those plans we've been talking about. How we'll be together, maybe get married, possibly even have kids. He's a lot older than I am, sure, but I know he'd make a great father.

I could just picture us going to parent-teacher conferences together. Sitting in the stands at our kid's soccer practice. Helping with homework or even just strolling down the sidewalk together on a sunny afternoon. Life will be so much better once he can finally tell his wife that he no longer wants to be with her. I just hope that day comes soon.

The smell of coffee and the sunshine from the window rises me. I'm surprised to see that I'm still on the couch. The TV is off and I can hear a sizzling skillet in the kitchen.

A smile comes across my face. Maybe last night was a dream. Maybe Malcolm actually did come over like he was supposed to.

I walk to the kitchen and try not to look disappointed when I see Tyler instead of Malcolm.

"Morning," he says brightly. "I hope you don't mind I used the last of your eggs. I'm making omelets."

"No, that's fine," I grumble in my morning voice. I cross the room and pour myself a cup of coffee, noting that he's still in the same clothes as last night. He must've spent the night. Odd. Why wouldn't he just go home when he lives right next door?

I shrug off the wonder and ask him, "You want a refill?"

He glances at his mug then holds it out to me with a smile. "Yeah, I could use one."

"What has you so happy this morning?" I top off his mug.

He shrugs and turns back to the skillet. "Oh, you know…just—it's morning. The day's still young."

I raise my eyebrows and nod once. "Right…" I take my cup of coffee to the small kitchen table and mix in a packet of sugar. "How long have you been awake?"

"Maybe half an hour." He points to the table. "I brought in the paper."

"Thanks." I pull it toward me and glance at the headline. *Montana Beach Pier opens for the season.* "Looks like Robyn is back at work."

"I saw that. Maybe she'll stop in sometime."

She's one of our best friends and the manager at the Montana Beach Pier amusement park, which is right next door to the Nine.

"You'd think she'd come more often when she's *not* working at the Pier." I take a careful sip of joe.

He laughs—a little too loudly—and says, "It's like she needs to walk by the Nine to remind her we're still around."

"Maybe. She does tend to do a lot of painting in the off season, so she's probably been busy with that."

"Oh, yeah. True. That's—that's probably what it was."

Why is Tyler acting weird this morning? And, more puzzling, why is he still here? I know he usually takes care of his mom in the mornings and yet he's making *me* breakfast.

Maybe I'm the reason. Maybe Tyler's—

No, that can't be it. Tyler's not gay. And I'm probably the one who knows the most about him. At the same time, though, everyone has secrets. I mean, look at me and Malcolm. Tyler doesn't know that he's married or really anything about him. In that regard, it's not too outrageous to think that Tyler has his own secret.

It would also explain why he spent the night. Of course, it's probably just that he's a good friend and wants to make sure that I'm still okay. I need more information.

"Where'd you sleep?" I ask abruptly.

"With you," he says, then adds quickly, "on the couch, that is. We fell asleep before the movie was over."

I nod. "And you didn't think to move somewhere else?"

He shrugs, his back to me still. "I guess I was comfortable."

"Guess so," I mutter. I decide it's probably best not to push my luck, so I add, "Yeah, I don't remember basically anything from that movie."

He laughs. "I gathered that because you started snoring within five minutes."

"I don't snore!"

"You were last night."

"If my snoring was so loud, why didn't you just go back to your house then?" Okay, that was too easy to pass up.

He turns away quickly and scoops up the omelets onto two plates. "It's ready!"

Taking the seat across from me, he sets our plates in front of us and digs into his food. We're quiet for a minute as we eat. It's good. I've never really had anything Tyler's cooked before, so it's a nice surprise. But then, he probably gets a lot of experience cooking for his mom nowadays. Kind of a bittersweet way to learn to cook.

"So are you feeling any better this morning?" he asks.

I shrug. "A little, yeah. A lot better than I would've been if you hadn't stayed. So thanks." I wonder if that's too much. If Tyler *does* have a thing for me, would a comment like that lead him on?

But I'm not exactly lying…

He smiles. "No problem. You know, if you really don't like being alone so much, maybe you should get a roommate. Or, at the very least, a dog."

I take a sip of my coffee. "I would *love* to get a dog. But I work too much and sleep too late. It wouldn't be fair. Not unless there was someone else to pick up the slack, you know?"

He nods and cuts into his food. "Yeah, I get it. I would love a dog too, but with everything going on lately, it'd be too much for Mom."

"I didn't realize you were a dog person."

"Are you kidding? A built-in best friend? Sounds good to me!" He looks up at me quickly and then looks down. "Not that I'm trying to replace you or anything."

That makes me smile. I might not have woken up to Malcolm, but it's still a good morning. How often do I wake up to breakfast waiting for me? I'm lucky to have a friend like Tyler.

"Thanks for making breakfast," I say. "It's really good."

"Thanks. I usually make my mom dinner before going to work, so I know my way around the kitchen. Plus, omelets are really easy."

Just what I thought.

"How's your mom doing?"

He shrugs. "About the same, you know? At this point, no news is good news. I'm just worried that things are going to tank really fast and Bailey and I aren't going to be prepared."

I make a face, but he doesn't look up from his food. "It's never convenient, but at least you're both there for her now. And you never know, she could recover."

He shakes his head. "She's not going to."

"Oh."

"Yeah." He scoops up the last of his food from his plate and looks at the clock. "Speaking of my mother, I should get going. Bailey has to get to work soon, which means I'm on mom-duty."

I watch him get up and cross the room to the sink. "Well, thanks for last night. And breakfast this morning. I really appreciate it. It's just what I needed."

Tyler smiles. "Well, I'm glad you're feeling better. I'll see you tonight at work?"

"I'll be there." I stand and we both hesitate, suddenly unsure of the best way to say goodbye. Do we hug? Wave? I'm very conscious of where my hands are and I slip them in the pockets of my shorts, but quickly decide that looks too forced, so I pull them out and cross my arms.

"Well, bye." He smacks my arm once and then turns away, nearly tripping over the chair he was just sitting in on his way out of the kitchen.

"Careful." I help him push in the chair.

"I guess I have to pay more attention," he says. "I'll

see you later." He grabs his shoes by the door and carries them with him when he leaves.

When he's gone, I blow out a long breath of air through pursed lips. I wonder what all of that was about. Is it just because I was vulnerable around him last night? But then, shouldn't *I* be the one feeling the most awkward? There has to be a better reason for his behavior than my half-baked theories.

I look at the dishes in the sink. I really should wash them, but I'm still tired. It's just after ten and I could go for another hour of sleep. In my bed, preferably.

Grabbing my blanket from the couch, I go back to my room, pull the blackout curtains closed, and collapse on the bed. I try to lose myself in thoughts of Malcolm and the future we'll have together, but Tyler's the one who sticks in my head.

He was really sweet to stay with me last night. I just wish I knew what was going on in his head. Or that I had the courage to just come right out and ask him. Maybe I'll find some courage tonight. Or maybe I can successfully forget about it and let things go back to normal between us. I'd like that.

My phone vibrates on the nightstand and startles me. I see it's Malcolm calling and quickly answer it.

"Can you talk?" It's how I've grown accustomed to answering the phone.

"Yeah, it's safe," he says. "I'm really sorry about last night. I was looking forward to spending the evening with you—I always am."

I smile and bury my head in the blanket as if he can see me. "I missed you, babe. When am I going to see you again?"

"Well actually, I was supposed to have a delivery in Texas that would take me two nights, but they canceled. My wife still thinks I have to go, though. I was thinking that I could spend it with you. All day, just you and me."

I smile wide. "Oh yeah?"

"I need to see you. I miss you like crazy. It's been a long time since we've had a day like that."

It has. The last time we saw each other during the day was a few months ago when his wife went to visit her sister in California for the week. That was one of the best weeks of my life with him. It was a perfect test run of what life will be like when it's just the two of us. We barely left the bedroom, though. Maybe this time that will be out of our system and we can do couple things. Take walks. Cook dinner. Just be together.

"That'll be nice." I daydream of the possibilities some more.

"We'll spend all day in bed," he says.

"Oh."

"You sound disappointed."

"Well, I just thought we'd do more than just…that."

"I can't help it with you. Besides, you can't deny that you're not thinking the same thing."

I blush and cover more of my face with the blanket.

He takes my silence as an admission. "That's what I thought. All day, babe, just you and me. We won't have to worry about my wife or work or anything for the day."

Work.

I sit up. "I can't tomorrow. I have to work."

He groans. "You do? You can't get out of it?"

"I'm the owner."

"Which means you can take off whenever you want."

I scrunch my brow. "Um, generally that means I work the most."

"Can't you just get two nights off? See if you can find someone to cover for you."

I consider it. I was going to do some of the inventory tomorrow, but I guess I can get a jump start on that tonight. And I might be able to swap shifts with someone.

"Okay," I say. "I'll see if I can get out of it for one night, at least."

"Not both?"

"No, I wouldn't feel right about that. It's such short notice."

"Okay. See what you can do. I can't wait to be with you, babe." I can hear the smile in his voice. "You're going to be in for such a good time."

"**I** was really looking forward to having tomorrow night off, though," Tyler says at work after I ask him to take my shift tomorrow night.

"*Please* Tyler?" I follow him into the stock room where he fills another case with liquor. "It's the only time he's free. We haven't had a day alone together in a long time—Malcolm and I, that is. Not you and me. We just—last night, I mean—uh, yeah."

Tyler turns away with a smirk.

"Anyway, you know how upset I was last night when he couldn't make it."

"What was his reason for that?"

"Oh, he, uh, had something at home that kept him."

Tyler lifts an eyebrow. "That's specific."

"It's personal."

"Okay."

"You say that as if you don't believe me."

He lifts up the filled case. "I believe you. I just think it was kind of shitty of him to bail on you at the last minute like that."

I shrug. "Something came up."

"And you're okay with that?"

"I don't really have a choice," I say. "It's not that big of a deal. It was just one night."

He shakes his head. "I don't know. I'm still not convinced."

"He said he was busy."

"And did he tell *you* what he was busy with? What was his personal reason?"

"For not coming?" I follow him out to the bar. There are a couple patrons already, but not too many.

"Yeah."

"Of course he told me."

"Are you okay with it?"

I hesitate. "Well…I guess so."

He sets the case down and starts emptying it. "You guess so? Adrian, you need to be sure."

"You just don't know him. And besides, I'm not asking for your approval, I'm asking for you to cover my shift."

That comment seems to sting. He doesn't look at

me. "I wanted a night off. I already told Bailey I could be with Mom."

"What if I made it up to you?"

"How?"

"Name your price."

"Really?" he asks. "Anything?"

"I mean, within reason."

"You said name my price."

I cross my arms. "Okay, fine. What is it? Anything at all."

Finally, he looks at me. "I want to meet Malcolm."

Chapter Four:
TYLER

"Why do you want to meet him?" Adrian asks.

"He's important to you. I'd like to get to know him."

He narrows his eyes and studies me. "Really?"

"Yeah." I finish unloading the box of liquor behind the bar. "Is that okay?"

He scratches the back of his head until I hand him the empty box. "Uh, I'll think about it."

"What are you so afraid of?"

"I'm not afraid," he says quickly. "It's just—I don't know if *he'd* be comfortable with it."

"Well, figure it out because your date is supposed to be tomorrow and *I* would like to know what I'm doing."

"I'll let you know."

We both watch as a large group of people come through the door and the hostess seats them in the corner.

"Looks like we're starting to get busy," Adrian says. "We'll talk after closing."

I fall into my usual routine, which is a balance between cleaning and serving until the dinner rush really starts to pile in. Everyone in the large group in the corner wants a cocktail, so I spend time making those while refilling beers at the bar.

For the most part, everyone who comes in is someone I recognize. Whether they're neighbors, relatives, friends, friends of friends, or just simply acquaintances, it's not hard to recognize people in a small town.

About an hour into my shift, I notice someone new walk in. He's blond and looks like he's lost in his own head. He takes in the bar, pausing to read the signs on the walls. He even looks up at the ceiling. Definitely a newbie.

Finally, he takes a seat at the bar and I set a cocktail napkin in front of him. "What can I get you?"

He looks over my shoulder at the drink menu on the wall. "Uh…whatever you recommend. I'm not picky."

This is always a trap. Most of the time, they *are* picky and if they don't like it, they usually don't want to pay for it. Especially out-of-towners like this. Luckily, this guy doesn't seem that threatening.

I grab a clean glass from underneath the bar and fill it. "This is called Atlantic Ale. Brewed up in North Beach. On the sweeter side, but not too bad."

"Thanks." He gives me a tight smile and plays with the corner of the cocktail napkin.

"Enjoy." I move to the end of the bar to get drinks for a group of girls all dressed up for a night out. I'm happy to see him pull a few bills out of his wallet. Either he likes it or he's just an overall honest person.

A little while later, I glance over and notice him staring at his drink with a glum expression. I move back to his end of the bar and ask, "So what's your deal, man?"

"What do you mean?"

"You look like your dog just died." I laugh. "You're kind of killing the mood."

"Sorry, just going through a lot of stuff."

"Care to share?"

"Not really."

"Mind if I vent a bit then?" I ask.

The whole Adrian and Malcolm thing bothers me. I can't help but feel like Adrian's rolling over for him—no pun intended. His hesitation at letting me meet

Malcolm is weird too. What's the big deal? Especially when he seemed so upset last night when Malcolm bailed at the last minute. That's not cool. Neither is the fact that I was a convenient replacement only when Adrian's evening opened up. I guess I have a lot of opinions on the subject.

But if I say any of this to Adrian, I know it'd come out all wrong.

"Isn't it supposed to be the other way around?" the blond asks. "Aren't you supposed to be the wise one?"

"Ha! You're funny." What was I thinking trying to vent to a customer who clearly has other things to worry about? I try to recover by playing it off. "Okay, fine. If you don't want to hear about my stuff, I won't tell you."

"Come on," he says. "You can spill if you want."

"No, it's okay. I won't burden you." This guy seems easy to talk to and since I know basically everyone else in here, I offer my hand. "I'm Tyler, by the way."

"Mason. Nice to meet you." He studies me and then asks, "Are you friends with Jessie Ray? From Montana Manor?"

"Am I friends with Jessie?" I roll my eyes and smirk. "Who *doesn't* know Jessie? Cute, blonde, kind of neurotic, but that's okay because we all love her."

We both laugh.

"Yeah, she's one of my best friends," I continue.

"I've known her since kindergarten, basically. You staying at the Manor, then?"

He nods. "Yeah, for two more weeks."

That would explain why I haven't seen him around before. And Jessie's a hard girl for new people to crack. If he's talking to her, they must be really close.

"So what brings you to this sleepy little town?" I wipe at the countertop to look like I'm working.

"A long vacation."

"And I take it the vacation isn't as relaxing as you thought it'd be?"

"It's not that. I'm having a great time."

"Oh yeah, I can tell." I grin. "Sorry. Go on."

"I just got a phone call from home and it wasn't a good one. Completely ruined my day. I ditched my date—at least, I think it was a date." He sighs. "Maybe it was. I don't know. Either way, I'm hungry and miserable. I probably should've just kept my original plans."

I wonder if Jessie is the date he ditched. It's a nice idea to know that she agreed to even *go* on a date—she hasn't been on one in quite a while—but I don't like it that she was ditched. If that's even the story. I need further information and if I'm going to get any kind of explanation out of him as to why—and whether she's *actually* the one he's been seeing—then I need to keep him here a bit longer.

"Well, I can't help you with your date or whatever's going on back home, but I can get you something to eat," I say. "On the house."

"You don't have to do that."

"Nonsense. The boss says to push the food to keep people here longer. Then they'll buy more drinks!" I flash him a smile and hope he buys it. Adrian doesn't like to give away free stuff, but if he's really that upset by it, he can take it out of my paycheck or something.

"Well, if that's the case, I could use another one of these." Mason lifts up his empty glass.

Mission One accomplished. Now on to Mission Two.

I give him a refill and go around to the kitchen to put in his order. Adrian nearly smacks me in the face with the door when I go to leave the kitchen.

"What the hell are you doing behind the door?" he asks with a chuckle. His feet start to carry him across the room, but I grab his arm to stop him.

"Hey, I need to tell you something."

"I'm busy." He shrugs out of my grasp. "Can't you tell me later?"

"No, I think it's about Jessie."

"Well, come get me when you know for sure."

"You're not the least bit interested in a guy who

might be dating Jessie?"

He looks out toward the bar and sighs. "What guy?"

"The one at the bar. Blond hair."

He takes a step back to peer out the kitchen door. "He's cute. What makes you think she's seeing him?"

"He asked if I knew her and he said he's staying at the Manor."

Adrian rolls his eyes. "It's an inn, not a whorehouse."

"I know *that*, but he mentioned that he kind of sort of had a date."

"Okay…"

"And Jessie's a single lady…"

"Tyler, the point?"

"She's our friend, don't you think we should feel him out in case he's just as bad as her ex?"

He looks back out at Mason. "Yeah, I suppose if he's bad news we should probably warn her."

"When was the last time you talked to Jessie?"

"It's been a while."

"So she hasn't mentioned this guy?"

Adrian cocks his head to the side. "Don't you think I would've told you if she had?"

"True. Well, I ordered him food on the house to see if I can get an explanation out of him."

He nods. "Free food for a guy who *might* be dating our friend and *might* have canceled their date?"

I roll my eyes. "You'll appreciate this more when you're not in the midst of the dinner rush."

"Which I really need to get back to." He pulls away from my grasp and moves through the kitchen.

When I return to the bar, I catch up on the waiting refills and process a couple orders. Thumping music starts to play, which signals the start of the evening crowd. I'm so busy that I don't get a chance to talk to Mason again until I see his order's ready.

He looks like he's about to get up when I set his plate in front of him. "Medium-well." I have to lean in close to him so he can hear. "If you need anything, let me know."

He mouths something, but I can't make it out over the noise of the music. I'm quickly whisked away to the other end of the bar where a crowd of people stand with cash in hand, ready to order drinks.

The number of people who come in keeps me busy for most of the rest of the night. It's nearly closing time by time I'm able to take a moment to catch my breath. I lean against the counter and sip a glass of water once the crowd has dispersed. It feels so good to take a break.

Mason is long gone. I didn't even see him leave. I would've thought he'd at least thank me for the free food.

I never did get more information out of him. Guess I should've made him pay.

By time the last customer has left, Adrian's started mopping the floor and I've already restocked the bar from the back. Again.

"It's been a busy night," I say to him once the banging music stops.

"We got lucky there," he says. "Thought I was going to have to call the cops."

"Why?"

"I'm going to go out on a limb here and say you were right. Jessie's seeing that guy—well, *was*."

"What happened?"

He leans on the end of the mop. "You didn't see? It was like three feet away from you!"

"No, I got so busy I wasn't really paying attention. What happened?"

"Jessie full on bitch-slapped that guy!"

"Really? Why?"

He shrugs. "No idea. She and Robyn took off right after she did it. He was chatting up some girl before that, though."

"Oh." I didn't even see that other girl. I wonder if that's why he called off the date. I can't imagine what she's going through. Her ex cheated on her and she was crushed. The fact that she smacked Mason isn't really surprising. And to think, I thought he was a good guy.

"Yeah," Adrian says. "I hope she's okay."

"Me too."

He resumes mopping. "Relationships are hard."

"I bet." I watch him finish up under the bar and then add, "Especially when you're hiding it from your best friends."

Adrian dunks the end of the mop in the bucket. "Are you still on that?"

"Do you still want me to work for you tomorrow?"

He sighs. "You're not going to let this go, are you?"

"Nope."

"It's *that* important to you?"

"Yup." Truth is, *he's* the one important to me. Not meeting Malcolm. But I'll keep that bit to myself. It's too awkward.

He chews on the inside of his cheek for a moment. "Okay, fine. You can meet him."

I smile. "Great! When?"

He shrugs and wheels the mop bucket back toward the closet. "I don't know, just sometime."

"I need a specific time and a place. The sooner the better. I know how he flakes out a lot."

He turns and shoots daggers with his eyes. "Low blow."

"Sorry."

"I can bring him tomorrow, I guess. During your shift. Maybe we'll have a drink, but nothing more. I don't want to get sucked up into work on my day off."

"Actually, it's *my* day off, but whatever."

He closes up the closet. "Thanks for covering for me. I really appreciate it."

"Sounds familiar. I believe you told me the same thing this morning."

He shoots a glance to the kitchen. "If you keep talking about that, people will start to think we're together."

My cheeks turn red and I look away. "Yeah, we wouldn't want that."

Bailey has the day off today, which means I'm not exclusively on mom-duty. After rolling over three or four different times in an attempt to sleep any later than ten, I decide it's no use and get up.

When I emerge from my bedroom, Mom and Bailey are watching TV in the living room.

"Morning." I step into the room long enough to give Mom a quick kiss and then escape back to the kitchen since she's lost in her show. I pour myself a bowl of cereal and lean against the counter to start eating when Bailey meets me in the kitchen.

"You can do what you want today," she says. "I'll take care of Mom. I promised her we'd play a couple games of euchre."

I nod and finish chewing. "Okay, but before you get busy with that, we should sit down to discuss the bills."

"Already?"

"Well, I've already been paying them," I say. "And the medical bills aren't going to let up anytime soon. I'd like to stay on top of them while we still have her insurance to cover it."

She looks away. "Uh, I don't know about today."

"Bailey, come on. This is the first time in a while that we're both home on your day off. Just give me half an hour so we can sort things out."

She takes a deep breath and looks back toward Mom. "Okay. When do you want to do that?"

"Let me go for a run and take a shower and then I'll be ready. Say, an hour?"

She nods. "Sure."

I finish my breakfast, head back to my room to pull on my sneakers, and debate whether I should text Adrian about tonight. I tell myself I'm not going to, but just before I hit *Play* on my running playlist, I type out a quick message.

D. Allen

Hey, don't forget to bring Malcolm tonight.

I tuck my phone away and press on with my run. When I get back, there aren't any new messages from anyone, which disappoints me. I try not to stress too much about it in the shower. Instead, I wrack my brain trying to think of everything I need to discuss with my sister.

When I get out, I grab the folder with everything in it and set it on the kitchen table. Mom's asleep in front of the TV and Bailey's playing on her phone on the couch.

"Hey," I murmur over the TV. "You ready?"

She doesn't say anything, but gets up and follows me to the kitchen. Instead of joining me at the table, though, she goes to the sink and turns on the water.

"What are you doing?" I ask.

"I just want to wash up these few dishes real quick," she says. "You can start. I'm listening."

"Bailey, I really need you to sit down and look at this."

She pushes up her sleeves. "I will later. Just give me the gist of it."

"Come on, I don't want to do this either, but we have to so we're not screwed once Mom goes."

"Oh, so this is to make your life easier after Mom dies?"

"Well, yeah," I say, noting her tone. "For both of us, actually. That way we both know what to expect."

"You just turn everything into a checklist, don't you?"

"I just want to make sure we have everything in order."

"And I think we'll be fine."

"Look, I know this isn't easy," I start, "but it's something we have to do. Mom's not getting any better. We'll inevitably have to deal with this. Better sooner than later."

"Oh, really? So let's start planning her death before there's even a sign that she's slipping away."

"Bailey, she has cancer. Everyone knows she's dying—Mom even knows she's dying. I'm just trying to think rationally about this."

"Are you even going to be sad when she goes?" She cuts the water and turns to face me. Her fingers drip all over the cabinets onto the floor.

"What are you talking about? Of course I will be."

"I have my doubts."

"Why?"

"All you care about is following some stupid routine."

I shoot a look to the living room to check to make

sure Mom's still asleep. Luckily, the TV is louder than we are.

"That's not true and you know it," I say. "I'm sorry you're having a hard time with this, but one of us needs to be strong so we're not drowning in bills when it's over."

She snatches a dish towel from the counter. "Whatever, do what you want. I don't want to think so morbidly."

I let her walk off. When the door to her bedroom slams, I close my eyes and let out a sigh. This is definitely not easy on any of us.

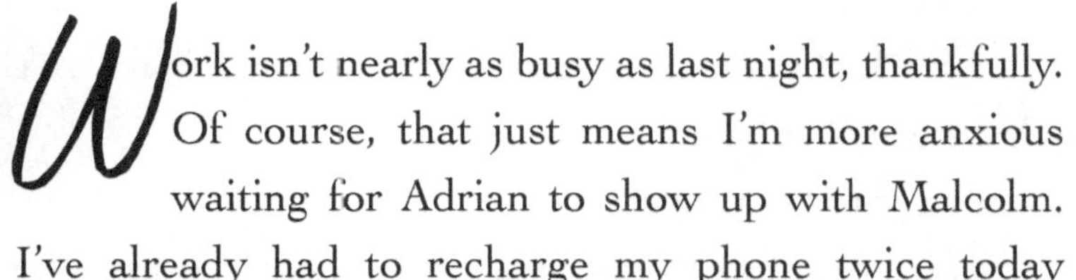

Work isn't nearly as busy as last night, thankfully. Of course, that just means I'm more anxious waiting for Adrian to show up with Malcolm. I've already had to recharge my phone twice today because I've killed the battery checking for a text from Adrian. Nothing. Not even in response to my reminder this morning.

I spend time making sure the bar is meticulously clean tonight. I suppose it's a compulsive disorder of some kind. The fact that it's so quiet doesn't help my mind from wandering.

I try to picture what Malcolm's like. No matter what type of person I envision, he doesn't measure up to someone who's good enough for Adrian. Especially not with what I already know about Malcolm. I just hope he doesn't flake out on Adrian again. I did *not* like seeing him cry.

"Hey buddy," the one lone customer left at the bar says. He's a middle-aged man who lives on Seventh Street. A frequent visitor, yet he refuses to learn our names. Then again, I don't know *his* name, either.

"Huh?" I look up from wiping the other end of the bar with a clean rag.

"I asked for a refill ten minutes ago."

"Oh, sorry." I step over and take his glass and fill it from the tap. "Here you go."

He looks at his glass and then at me. "This isn't what I was drinking."

I scrunch my eyebrows. "It isn't?"

He rolls his eyes and shakes his head. "Whatever, I'll drink it."

"Sorry," I repeat.

I resume cleaning up the bar, trying to act casual in case Adrian and Malcolm come in.

Really, I wish it was just Adrian coming. I wouldn't mind Malcolm going away. I just don't want Adrian to be as upset as he was the other night. I wish Malcolm was never a blip on his radar. But he is, so I need to deal with it. I can't push Adrian away because I don't get good vibes from what he tells me about his boyfriend. Especially since I've never even met the guy.

Just after midnight, I text Adrian to remind him—again. The bar has mostly emptied out. Rick, our most frequent regular, is the only one still here. He seems content watching the news at the opposite end of the bar with a drink in his hand.

Finally, just when I think for the millionth time that he's not coming, I see Adrian on the other side of the door.

Relief washes over me. I smile and come around the bar to greet him but stop short when an older man follows him in. My heart sinks to my stomach and I force myself to keep the smile on my face.

"You made it," I say as cheerfully as I can manage.

"Yeah, it took a little convincing," Adrian says. He looks back at the older man and says, "Uh, this is Tyler." Adrian motions to me and then to the man. "And this is Malcolm."

I step forward to shake Malcolm's hand. He's tall, which distracts from his large beer belly. His silver hair seems to stand out against his tan skin and when he smiles, deep laugh lines spread across his face.

"Nice to finally meet you," I say, making sure my

grin is still plastered on. "Adrian's said he's been seeing someone for a while now, so it's nice to finally put a face to a name."

Malcolm nods. "I've heard a bit about you. You're his employee, right?"

I look over at Adrian, who's red in the face, and then back at Malcolm. "Only on paper. So what did you guys do today? Anything fun?"

Malcolm looks around, apparently without hearing me—even though he heard me before. Adrian looks down and lets out a quiet chuckle.

Message received.

"Oh, I see."

Malcolm scratches his beard and as he moves his hand, the light catches the reflection of something on his hand.

A wedding ring.

Chapter Five:
ADRIAN

"I'm going to show Malcolm the beach," I say. "He's never been to it."

Tyler looks startled. "Oh, um, okay—wait, haven't you guys been dating for a while now? And he's *never* seen the beach?"

I look down as another nervous smile breaks across my face. I don't think it's ever going to be easy talking to Tyler—or anyone—about my relationship with Malcolm. Not when it's always been a secret.

"I mean, he shouldn't have said never, but we usually don't make it as far as the beach," Malcolm says.

Tyler nods once, not quite meeting Malcolm's eyes. He turns and looks back at the nearly-empty bar. "Well, I should start cleaning up before we close. It's been a long day and I really just want to get home and sleep."

Right. He feels awkward too. Good thing we're not staying for a drink, even though I promised him we would. Only making a quick appearance was the only way I could get Malcolm to come at all. I didn't think he'd object to the idea of coming to the bar, but I guess I was wrong.

I mean, I can't blame him. We have limited time together so we should spend it *together*. It's not that I don't want to see Tyler, but the alone time I have with Malcolm—which is precious tonight since I don't have to share him with his wife—is too tempting to waste any more of it.

"Thanks again for covering for me," I tell Tyler as I lead Malcolm to the patio door to the beach. "I'll see you later."

Tyler moves behind the bar and doesn't look up when we leave.

I don't know what his deal is when *he* asked to meet Malcolm, but I push it out of my mind. This weekend is another glimpse of what life is going to be like when it's just me and Malcolm. I need to take advantage of it.

I reach for Malcolm's hand once we're alone. He pulls it away quickly and stuffs it in his pocket.

"What's the matter?" I ask.

"Not out in the open like this," he mutters.

I motion to the empty beach. "There's no one around."

He points to the buildings on the edge of the beach. "Someone could be looking."

"You're being paranoid."

"I'm being safe."

"You didn't have a problem just now at the Nine."

He exhales loudly. "That was different."

"How?"

"We could've been just friends."

I look down at my feet as we walk across the sand. "You made it pretty obvious that we weren't *just friends*. And I thought you were okay with some people knowing?"

He shakes his head. "You and your friend are the only ones who know about us. And now that guy that was sitting at the bar."

"Rick? He wasn't paying attention."

"You don't know that."

I bite my lip because I don't want to argue with him. Not when this was supposed to be our special time alone together.

"Well, can we at least sit and enjoy the view for a while?" I ask.

He looks around, then turns back to me. "You're the only view I need."

"Babe, that's not what I meant. I just want to sit with you and watch the waves for a bit."

"But you're more beautiful than any wave." He steps closer with that familiar look of lust in his eyes. Not too close in case anyone—heaven forbid—thinks we're together. "I could watch you all day." He tugs at my baby blue button up shirt. "Too bad you're covering such a masterpiece."

I roll my eyes and laugh. "Okay, *that* was cheesy."

"It's your fault."

"No, *this* is my fault." I grab his arm and start to pull him toward the water, but he whips it away from my grasp, knocking me to the ground.

"I said no!" His voice carries across the empty beach.

I stare up at him with wide eyes. This is a side of him I haven't ever seen before. I don't like it.

Malcolm's face immediately softens and he offers his hand. "I'm so sorry, babe. Are you okay?"

I brush the sand off of me and get to my feet on my own. "I'm fine."

"I would just rather be alone with you, that's all. Maybe get you out of those clothes and into something more—"

"We've already done it once today," I snap. "You really want to do it again?" I'm not sure I'm up for that, but I don't want to disappoint him. And this *is* supposed to be our special night. I want to make him happy.

He smiles. "I think you know the answer to that."

I look out at the ocean. There's no moon, so the stars litter the sky. It looks beautiful. I wish we could just lay in the sand and listen to the waves crash on the beach. Forget about the world and everyone in it and just *be*. Together. But I realize I'm not going to win this fight. Malcolm would rather go home.

"Okay, we can go back," I murmur.

"I swear, I'll make it up to you, babe."

As we get moving, though, we both walk in silence. Malcolm's hands are firmly planted in his pockets and he marches at such a fast pace that I nearly need to jog to keep up.

I know I shouldn't complain about him during the few times we're together, but sometimes I wish we could act like we're an actual couple. Outside of the bedroom. Even if it's just simply holding hands or meeting each other's friends.

I guess he *did* just meet Tyler, so that's a step in the right direction. I suppose I can't ask more from Malcolm yet if he's not ready. Everyone needs to be able to come out on their own terms. I can't push him. I have to have patience.

We get back to my house and I fumble with the

keys in the dark. Malcolm must feel more comfortable now that we're nearly inside because he's reaching around me and unbuttoning my shirt.

When I swing the door open, he pushes me inside and presses me against the back of the door. He kisses me like he hasn't seen me in weeks. Like we haven't been together since he first pulled in the driveway this morning. Like we haven't been in nearly this exact position several hours ago.

Without a word between us, he leads me to the bedroom where the bulk of our relationship takes place. He moves with a sense of hunger and I realize that even if this relationship isn't perfect, I should be happy that someone looks at me the way Malcolm does. That somebody wants me like he does. That somebody loves me like he does. If it weren't for him, I'd probably be alone.

I roll over the next morning and bump into Malcolm. I groan. I'm not used to sharing the bed in the mornings. That's about the only perk of Malcolm usually never staying the night, which is something I just realized. But he's here, so I have to enjoy it.

He turns to face me and his eyes open as slits at

first until they adjust to the muted morning light threatening to sneak in through the curtains.

"Morning." He reaches for me and pulls me close so our naked bodies are smushed together.

"Morning, babe," I say. A moment later, I add, "This is nice."

It's the first time in long time that we've woken up together. I should take full advantage. I don't even try to guess what time it is or even think about working later tonight. I'm here with him right now and that's all that should matter. I should feel lucky.

"Mmm, it is." He releases me and lifts up the covers to look at my body. "You look nice, too. Wore just what I wanted."

I shake my head with an eye roll. "You mean nothing?"

"That's it." He kisses me. Bad morning breath between us both, but it doesn't matter. He's here and we're together. This is what I've always wanted, isn't it?

He sneaks his hand inside the blanket and down the side of my body.

I push it away. "Stop. I just want this." I lean forward to kiss him, but he backs away.

"That's a bit of a tease, don't you think?"

"What?"

"Kissing without anything else after."

"Babe, we did it twice yesterday. Let's give it a break. Take a day off."

"Why do you think I drove all this way?" he says.

I sit up on my elbow. "I *thought* it was to see me."

He notices that I'm miffed and he changes his expression. "No, of course I want to see you. You're right. I just want to show you how much I love you." He kisses my shoulder and down my chest. I pull away from him, slink back down on the mattress, and pull the covers to my chin.

"I know you love me," I say. "I love you, too. But it's okay if we don't have sex one day."

He pushes himself against me. "But I don't know if I can handle that. We have one more night together and I don't want to waste a second of it. You're already going to leave me tonight for work."

"I couldn't take *two* days off in a row. I'm the owner and one of the few employees. I kind of need to be there."

"I know, but I just wish you'd make it up to me while we still have the time."

I'm quiet as I consider what he's saying. I guess he has a point. He'll be waiting a long time for me while I'm at work. I should give him a little something this morning. Even if I'm not in the mood. It's not like it'll be the end of the world.

"Okay, but just a quick one," I say.

Malcolm smiles wide. "I'd rather take my time with you."

Almost as soon as we're done, Malcolm's off in the bathroom to take a shower. I lie in my bed and cover myself in the blankets. That did not feel good. I should've just said no and meant it. I wish I wouldn't have given in to his persistence.

He comes out of the shower after a while and I bury my head under my pillow. He rubs my back and asks, "Hey, what's the matter?"

I pull the blanket tighter but don't say anything. I just want him to leave me alone until I feel better. About everything.

"Are you going to take a shower?"

It doesn't even take any effort not to say or do anything. It's almost like I'm broken. I'm content to lay like this forever.

"Look, babe, I have to run back to work for a little bit to check on things. The wife may think I'm gone, but the boss still knows I'm off. If I don't go in, they're going to start calling the house." He continues to rub my back. It helps. Maybe he feels bad about not listening. "Can you at least say goodbye?"

I roll over and look at him. "You're leaving? I thought we were going to spend the day together?"

"I wish we could, but I have stuff to take care of," he says, flashing me a smile now that I'm talking to him again. As if everything's all right. "I meant to tell you last night, but we got back kind of late and, you know, *got busy*." He smiles and runs his fingers gently along my skin.

I roll away from his touch and bury my face in the blanket again. "If you knew last night, why didn't you tell me until just now?"

"I don't know, babe, I guess I didn't think it was that important." He tries to pull me back around to face him. "Come on. I'll make it up to you when I get back tonight."

"Without sex?" I successfully shrug off his attempts to roll me over.

"Since when don't you like sex?"

"Since just now."

"You didn't like that?"

No is on the tip of my tongue, but I can picture the look of pain he'd have on his face if I told him that. I can't do that to him. No matter how angry I am.

Instead, I roll over again and look at him. "Not tonight. I mean it this time."

He nods. "Okay. I promise. Can I at least have a kiss?"

I close my eyes and purse my lips until I feel his press against mine.

"I'll wait up for you when you get out of work." He stands and crosses the room to the door. "Get up and take a shower. It'll make you feel better."

"Okay, I'll see you tonight."

Maybe constantly being together isn't the best for any relationship. Maybe maintaining a certain level of independence is better. Maybe that's all this is. Growing pains over the course of our relationship.

I look up and see Malcolm lingering by the door. "I love you, babe."

"I love you, too."

Chapter Six:
TYLER

"That's all I could find on this guy," Adrian says into the phone in the office when I get into work. "Yeah, you're probably right… Okay… Sorry I can't help you out. I hope it's a huge success for you guys… Uh-huh. You too. Bye!"

"Who was that?" I clock in at the tablet mounted on the wall.

"Jessie. She's having a Fourth of July party at the Manor." He doesn't take his eyes off the computer as he clicks around.

"That's new."

He grabs a pen and scribbles on a pad of paper. He seems surprised to see I'm still standing here when he looks up. "Huh? Oh. Yeah, it is."

I lean forward against the back of the extra chair. "You're here early."

"It's a good thing, too," he says with his head down on the pad of paper while he writes. "Otherwise, I would've missed Jessie's call."

I tilt my head out toward the bar. "Actually, Robyn texted me earlier and asked if she could stop by for lunch. I thought it couldn't hurt to come in a little early myself, so I said it was fine."

"Okay," he says, not paying much attention to me. "I'll be out in a minute. I'm just figuring out tonight's specials."

I step toward the door, but hesitate. "Are you okay?"

He finally looks up and flashes a smile. "Of course I am, why wouldn't I be?"

I shrug. "I don't know. I just thought you'd want to spend more time with Malcolm."

Adrian returns to what he's working on. "Oh. He had to run to work for a bit."

"Even though he knew you were looking forward to it?"

He runs his hands over his face. "Why don't you just say it?"

"Say what?"

"That you don't like him."

"I didn't—I don't even know him."

"But you're already judging him."

I rock my head back and forth while I think of the best way to respond. "I'm nervous about him."

Adrian crosses his arms and sits back, expecting a further explanation from me.

"He's our parents' age. Isn't that weird?" I ask.

"No, because we're both grown adults who are mature enough to look past it."

I consider dropping it and just letting him do what he wants, but it doesn't feel right with me. And the fact that Adrian's so defensive about it tells me that deep down it doesn't sit well with him, either.

"Adrian…he's married, isn't he?"

He looks away.

I let out a heavy sigh and pinch the bridge of my nose. "What are you doing with him?"

"We love each other, okay? It's as simple as that."

"Okay…" I try to decide what else to add without insulting him.

"He's going to leave his wife."

"Oh, so he's separated?" Maybe it's not as bad as it sounds.

"Not exactly."

"Does his wife know about you?"

He closes his eyes. "No."

"Okay," I repeat.

"See, you're judging."

"I'm not!"

"You think I'm some slut trying to break up a marriage!"

"Adrian, cool it! I didn't say anything like that. I just—" Deep breath. Regroup. Retry. "Okay, you love him. I get it. Does he love you back?"

He nods. "Absolutely."

Are you sure? Is on the tip of my tongue but I don't voice it. "Has he met with a lawyer or someone to file for divorce?"

He looks away again. "I don't know."

"But he stills plans on leaving her?"

"He promised me he was."

"How long has he been promising you that?" I ask quietly.

Adrian opens his mouth to retort, but Robyn's voice calls us from the bar.

"We're in here," I shout back to her before Adrian can say anything. I turn to the door, but look back at him just before I leave. We study each other, trying to determine what the other is thinking.

"Am I too early?" Robyn steps toward the office.

I come through the door and try to sound cheery. "Not at all. Are you having your usual? Turkey club on wheat, no onion?"

She nods. "Yeah, if that's okay. I don't want to put you guys out."

"Don't worry about it. I'll get working on it. Take a seat at the bar. We'll be out in a minute." I cross the room to the kitchen and put together her sandwich. I usually try to stay out of the kitchen, but the cooks for the day aren't here yet.

Once her sandwich is all made, I pull a clean plate from the dishwasher and set her food on it. I pull a pickle out of one of the containers in the fridge and add it to the plate.

As I carry it back out, I say, "Order up!"

"Oh, thanks!" Robyn picks it up and takes a bite.

Adrian's standing on a stool behind the bar writing the drink specials on the chalkboard display. I sneak around him, making myself as small as possible, and start washing the glasses in the sink.

"So what's been new with you?" Adrian asks over his shoulder. He looks down at a notepad before writing the next special on the board.

"Just working at the Pier," she says around a mouthful.

"Any new employees?" I ask.

She sets the second half of the sandwich down and wipes her mouth. "Three, yeah. They're not bad."

"You mean they're not completely incompetent?" I

grin at her to show I'm joking.

She cringes. "Yeah, I guess I am pretty critical of the newbies."

"Try everyone," Adrian adds.

"I'm not that bad." She takes a bite of her pickle.

Bailey is one of Robyn's employees and has had her share of rants about my friend.

"Everyone at the Pier seems to think so." Once the words come out, I realize how harsh it sounds, but there's no time to take them back.

"They all hate me anyway," she says.

Adrian turns around and smirks at her. "I'm sure there's *someone* there who doesn't hate you."

"What do you know?" she nearly shouts.

I look between them. "What? What's going on?"

"Robyn's got a man-friend," he teases.

"Where did you hear that?" Robyn leans across the bar toward Adrian.

He laughs and gets down from the barstool. "Okay, don't freak out. It's not that big of a deal. Jessie called to ask about providing beverages for her party tomorrow—which I can't because the liquor license is restricted to this building—but she mentioned that you had a date with someone from the Pier."

"Oh." She falls back into her seat and looks down at her plate.

I smile at her. "Oh? That's all we get? Who is this mystery man?" What kind of friend would I be if I didn't tease my friends?

"One of her employees," Adrian says in Robyn's silence. "Based off a preliminary Facebook search, I found that he's single, a graduate of the Art Institute of Charleston, and really cute."

"You found all that from just his first name?" she asks.

"It's not like his name is Bob," he says. "There are only so many Jadens who work at the Pier. Actually, he's the only one."

"Oh, his name is Jaden?" I turn off the water and grab a towel to dry my hands.

"You've gotta give us something, otherwise we'll have to ask around for more details," he says.

Robyn groans and I steal a glance at Adrian, who smiles back at me. At least we didn't completely ruin our friendship with that fight. And it's nice that he said 'we' as in me and him.

"Last night was only our second date and it's still very new," she says after a moment. "If you ruin this I'm going to kill you."

Adrian puts up his hands in surrender. "I don't have any intentions of ruining it for you. I just want to know the details of what's happening in one of my best friend's love life."

"Jessie's? Is she still with Mason?" Robyn picks at the bread on her sandwich.

"We're talking about you," I say.

Honestly, at this moment, I'm not that interested in Robyn's story. But I keep pressing her for more because I like this dynamic that's developed between me and Adrian. Hopefully it's a sign that we'll be okay even if I'm skeptical about his boyfriend.

She takes another bite of her sandwich. Adrian looks at his watch and then crosses his arms.

"We don't open for another few hours, so we have time," he tells her. "If you want any more pre-opening food, you better spill."

"Okay, here it is: we went on a date because he kept helping me out at work," she says.

"Bribery?" I ask. "That seems like it's crossing a line." Ugh, that was judging. I suck in my bottom lip and make a conscious effort not to look at Adrian until the moment passes.

Luckily, he makes a joke of it. "It doesn't take much for you, does it?" He moves to the sink to wash the chalk off his hands.

"It's not like that," she says quickly. "He asked me out. I like talking to him, so I said yes. But then when we were having ice cream—"

"*That* was your date? Robyn…" Adrian clucks his

tongue and shakes his head.

I cross my arms and lean against the counter, trying not to think of what kind of dates Adrian and Malcolm go on. From what I could tell from last night, they don't *go* anywhere.

"It was really hot that day!" she cries out.

"I'm sure *somebody* was burning up," he mutters, drying his hands in a towel.

She pushes on despite his jokes. "Anyway, I saw Peggy while we were out."

Peggy's her assistant at the Pier. According to Bailey, she's kind of lazy. Just like a lot of the employees there. No wonder they all hate Robyn, who makes them do actual work.

"She didn't see us, but I hid anyway," she continues. "Jaden was mad. Thought I was embarrassed to be seen with him."

"Are you?" I ask.

"No! I was just afraid that we would both lose our jobs if Peggy told the owners and that it'd look…well, *you know*." She pauses, but neither of us say anything. "The rest of the workers already hate me. This would be just another reason."

"Sounds like you're overthinking this just a tiny bit," Adrian says.

"Maybe. Anyway, I apologized to Jaden and had

him over for dinner last night—"

"Oooo," Adrian says as if he was hurt.

"What?"

"Your cooking could use some work."

"They were salads," she says.

He raises his eyebrows. "That's…romantic."

I smack him, hoping that he doesn't take offense to it. I never had to wonder what he thought before. Now I do. Something's definitely off between us.

"Ignore him," I tell her. "What did Jaden think?"

She shrugs. "He seemed to like it. Anyway, afterwards we went out to the hammock and, well…" Her cheeks turn red.

Adrian giggles. "That's my girl!"

Yup, I definitely know what type of dates he and Malcolm have.

"Nothing happened!" she says quickly. "Well, not *that*."

I force a smile. "So you had a good time?"

"Yeah, and I really like him but…"

"What?" I ask.

"I don't know." She shrugs. "I'm his boss. That's crossing a line. And he's younger than me—"

"Age gaps are *not* that big of a deal," Adrian says quickly.

I glare at him. I'm not sure what it is exactly, but I

just wish everything was different. That Adrian and Malcolm weren't together. That he wasn't so hooked on someone who seems like he's just using him. That Adrian could see what I see.

I can feel Robyn's eyes on us, but she just presses on about Jaden. "Okay, so the age thing isn't really what's bothering me. I mean, it's only five years, but I guess I just have this feeling that it's…wrong."

I shake my head. "It's not wrong if you're happy."

"I agree." Adrian looks hard at me.

That's not what I meant at all, but I don't want to contradict myself in front of Robyn — or shine a light on what's going on in Adrian's love life.

"What's going on with you two?" she asks.

I look out at the empty room. "Nothing," I say more harshly than I intend.

"Okay then."

Adrian leans on the counter and holds Robyn's hands. "Do you like him?"

"I do."

"Then don't worry about the rest."

I lean against the counter and close my eyes, trying not to think about that being Adrian's reasoning for sleeping with a married man. A man who is probably only with him for sex. But just like what I said to Robyn earlier that Adrian picked up on, this isn't about him and

Malcolm. It's about Robyn and Jaden.

"Jessie thinks we might be better off waiting until the summer's over," Robyn says. "When he's not my employee anymore. He'll probably move back to North Beach, though."

"The summer will only last so long," I say. "Don't put off something that could be really great. Take advantage of it now."

Rich words coming from someone like me. I should just tell Adrian what I really think.

"Yeah, you're right," she admits.

"When's your next date?" I ask.

"Tonight. But I also kind of want to spend tomorrow with him too, since it's the Fourth," she says. "The fireworks, the stars, lying in the grass. It seems romantic."

"Aw, it does!" Adrian says.

"What about Jessie's party?" I ask. "We have to work tomorrow, so we can't go. One of us should probably be there to support her." We all have a lot going on, but we can't ignore Jessie in the process. She has a lot going on, too.

Robyn makes a face. "Oh yeah. I forgot. I also have to work."

"You'll be done by time the fireworks start," Adrian says.

She exhales loudly. "Yeah, I guess."

"Jessie's been kind of MIA since she's been with this new guy," I add. "What's going on with that?"

"Are they still together? What happened after she bitch-slapped him here?" Adrian asks Robyn, still too perturbed to look at me.

"They argued a bit on the street—stuff with her ex, mostly," she explains.

Adrian and I both nod in acknowledgement. Jessie's fiancé cheating on her was just one of the many reasons she moved back to Montana Beach.

"Then we went back to her place and when I finally got her to calm down, I convinced her to try to talk to him to hear him out," Robyn adds. "I don't know if she has, though. I haven't texted her. I probably should."

"Especially if you're going to ditch her tomorrow," I say.

"Yeah." She looks at the time on her phone. "I should probably get going. There are some errands I want to run on my way home, plus I want to get something done on that landscape I've been working on."

A new painting, presumably. There are a couple of her pieces hanging here at the Nine.

"Besides," she continues, "you guys probably have to get ready to open. Thanks for listening—even if you did drag it out of me."

Adrian smiles. "That's what we do."

After Robyn leaves, I reach for her plate and take it back to the kitchen to clean it. While I'm back there, I try to think of the best thing to say to Adrian that would test the waters to see if there's any residual tension from our argument earlier.

Are we good? Too direct.

Do you need help with anything? Not direct enough.

Can we talk? What if he thinks everything is fine?

When I come out of the kitchen, though, he's gone. The light in the office is on but I can't build up the courage to go back there and talk to him. What would I say without it looking desperate? Or weird? Or like I can't let it go?

I'll just give him space for now. I'll talk to him later.

I pull out the cleaner and start dusting off the shelves. It's busywork, especially since this place was spotless the other night, but it has to be done again. Especially before customers come, who might be allergic to the cleaner.

After the bottles are all cleaned off, I go to the cleaning closet next to the office door and pull out the mop. Might as well clean the floors really good in the daylight. As I start to wheel it out to the restaurant, though, Adrian comes out of the office.

"Hey," he says.

"Hey, look—"

"Could you—" he says at the same time.

We both stop.

"You go," he says.

"No, it's nothing. What were you going to say?"

He clears his throat. "Could you, uh, wipe down the tables out on the patio?"

I look out toward the beach and nod. "Sure, no problem."

"Thanks."

He goes to the bar and grabs the cleaner and I start mopping while he cleans the windows. I'm almost done mopping the floor when Frankie comes in.

"Good afternoon, boys," he says.

Adrian follows him into the kitchen and I can hear them talking about things to do before the dinner rush comes.

I finish up mopping, pack it away in the closet, and move out to the patio tables. I'm just finishing up when the first diners arrive for dinner. I hand them some menus and seat them in the corner. Table 12. The waitress should be here anytime now.

Behind the bar, I fill their water glasses when Adrian comes over.

"Did they order yet?" he asks quietly.

I shake my head. "Not yet."

"Okay. Hopefully Carrie will be here soon."

"Yup."

As the dinner rush picks up, I don't get a chance to talk to Adrian again, but I watch as he busies himself with any task he can think of. Vacuuming the office, checking inventory in the stock room, seating customers.

It's not until the thumping music stops at closing and we're walking out for the night that we're alone. We don't say anything to each other as he locks up and we head back down the sidewalk toward home.

Just like the other night, Adrian buries his nose in his phone as we walk. When we turn onto Atlantic Street from First Street, the silence is driving me nuts.

"So tonight was busy," I say.

"Yeah."

"Did we make a lot of money?"

He shrugs. "Decent."

"That's good." We keep on walking for a bit. It's a wonder he doesn't trip on the cracking sidewalk with his attention solely on his phone.

"I'm sorry for judging Malcolm based on his age," I blurt.

He looks up at me, startled. "Oh. Thanks."

I consider mentioning the fact that Malcolm's married, but I'm not sorry for my concern about that. I don't want to say something I don't mean. Malcolm *should* leave his wife before he starts seeing someone else—especially if that someone is Adrian.

"Is he coming over tonight?" I ask.

Adrian keeps his eyes on his phone. "He should already be there. He said he'd wait for me when I got home."

"Gotcha."

We walk on a little farther. The silence isn't any better. Adrian hasn't said much, which is killing me more than if we were arguing. I wish I knew what he thought of our disagreement. Whether he's mad at me. Whether I'm even on his mind at all.

Adrian's phone dings again, but it's different this time. His shoulders slump and he lets out a heavy sigh.

"What?" I ask.

He shakes his head and keeps walking. "Nothing."

I grab his arm to stop him. "No, what is it? Is it Malcolm? He's not coming, is he?"

When he looks at me with sad eyes, my insides melt.

"No, he's not."

Chapter Seven:
ADRIAN

All my insecurities about Malcolm seem to flood me in this moment and before I realize it, my shoulders start to shake as the tears pool out of my eyes.

Tyler rubs my back. "Hey, it's okay. Maybe he got busy or something."

I sniffle. "No, he does this all the time. He gets what he wants and—" I stop myself. I can be mad at him, but I can't vilify him like that. For all I know he *did* get busy. I have to cut him some slack. Especially in front of Tyler, who already has some misconceptions about Malcolm.

Surprisingly, Tyler doesn't say anything else for a

while. He just continues to rub my back and waits for me to calm down, which I don't. Ordinarily, I'd be embarrassed about crying over a guy on the street in the middle of the night like some cheesy rom-com, but it's Tyler and I know he just wants me to feel better.

Actually, I'm glad he's here. On nights like these when Malcolm bails on our plans, it's the quiet that's the hardest part to get through. It seems to only echo my loneliness.

"Come on," Tyler finally says.

"What?"

"We're going on a little trip."

I'm confused. "It's the middle of the night."

"I know, which is why this is the perfect time." He starts walking again and looks back at me still frozen where we stopped. "Just trust me."

I decide to take his advice and follow him back home. It's not like I was expecting to get to sleep right away anyway. A little ride might actually distract me.

He gets in the old pickup truck that's always parked in his driveway. It's the one he and his grandpa worked on before he died.

I follow his lead and get in the passenger side. When he fires up the engine and starts driving out of town, I ask, "Where are we going?"

Tyler looks over at me and smiles. "You said you

were going to trust me."

I look out the window as we whiz by the houses just outside of town in the expanse of marshes. Soon we're driving by farm fields on either side of the road, divided only by barriers of trees and brush. I glance at the clock and watch time tick past until we've been driving for nearly twenty minutes.

I'm about to ask him again where we're going, but he pulls off onto a dirt road down a wooded path. I hold onto the handle above the door as the truck rocks back and forth over the potholed road.

At the end, we turn left into an open field. Bails of rolled hay are scattered around us. Tyler drives into the middle and cuts the engine.

"What is this?" I ask.

"A friend of our family owns it and rents it to one of the farmers out here." He looks over at me. My nerves must be showing because he chuckles. "Relax, it's not trespassing. He said I could come whenever I wanted."

"But why are we here? What are we doing?"

He rolls down the window with the crank and hangs his arm out. "We're enjoying the quiet."

I look around. Not only is it absolutely silent besides the crickets, but everything's so still. Peaceful, even.

The metal door complains as he opens it. "Come on, we should be able to get a good view of the stars out here." He grabs an old blanket from behind the bench seat and slams the door shut.

I get out with a similar squeak of the door and watch as he drops the tailgate and fans out the blanket in the bed of the truck.

He hoists himself up onto the bed and lies down on his back. "Wow."

My head immediately looks up and I nearly say the same thing. In every direction there are more stars than I ever thought possible. More than I saw on the beach last night. *A lot* more. They fill the sky like an endless undiscovered ocean. Even with just the quickest glance, I'm completely captivated.

"Come here," Tyler says. "So you don't have to crane your neck."

I hop up in the bed of the truck and lay next to him. I fold my arm under my head and stare up at the sky. I could get lost in this. I wonder if Robyn has ever painted anything like this. I wonder if she's even *seen* anything like this. I certainly haven't. Even in a small little town like Montana Beach, there's too much light.

"This is beautiful," I say to Tyler. "Thanks for bringing me."

"I thought it'd cheer you up."

"How often do you come here?" I keep my eyes on the sky.

"Not a lot anymore. Not since Mom's been sick. She used to bring me and Bailey out here every week when she could."

I look over at him, but he's still looking up. "I'm really sorry your mom's sick. How's she doing?"

"It's okay. She's hanging in there, I guess. Definitely puts things into perspective, doesn't it?"

"How so?"

"Life is too short to not do what makes you happy." He looks over at me. "Or to be with someone who doesn't make you happy."

I look up again, not ready to talk about Malcolm. Rather, not wanting to hear a *lecture* about him. Not yet, at least.

"So your mom's really not going to get any better?"

"No," he says softly.

I move my arm over until it's pressed against his and squeeze two of his fingers. "I'm really sorry."

He's quiet. I don't look over at him. He probably doesn't want to talk about this. Just like I don't want to talk about Malcolm. Well, okay, it's not *exactly* the same thing.

He pulls his hand away from mine and wipes at his face. "This is so stupid," he says. "We've known for a while that this was coming."

"It doesn't make it any easier," I say. He's crying and it feels like there's a vice grip around my heart. I hate seeing him like this.

"No, I guess not."

"What does she think about it?"

He wipes his nose. "She's okay. She says she's lived a good life, that she's taught me and Bailey a lot. Obviously, she wishes she had more time—we all do—but she's happy with the time she's had with us."

I look over at him. "At least she's staying positive."

He lets out a heavy breath. "Yeah. The problem is Bailey."

"She's not taking it so well?"

"No. And she thinks that I'm taking it *too* well."

"Why?" I ask.

"I'm just trying to be prepared for life after Mom's gone, but Bailey thinks I'm being morbid. I'm just trying to be rational!"

"Everyone grieves differently. Just give her some time. I'm sure she'll be grateful when the time comes."

"Yeah."

I watch as he wipes at his eyes again in an effort to dry them. I hope I helped make him feel better. Not that there's anything I can say that will make the situation any better.

I look back up at the stars. The crickets fill the space between us. If I close my eyes, I'm sure I'd fall asleep easily. I'm safe. I'm content. I'm laying here next to my best friend in a quiet, secluded field. It's perfect.

The night turned out to be better than I thought it would. Well, minus Tyler crying. That was certainly not a highlight.

"Can I ask you something?" Tyler says quietly.

I know what's coming. I can almost feel it in my chest. But I just asked him about a tough subject. I suppose I should open up about mine. "Yeah."

"How did you meet Malcolm?"

I close my eyes and the memory comes back to me instantly. "It was at the small business conference I go to every year in North Beach. He was there representing his trucking company."

"How does his trucking company relate to your bar?"

"It doesn't. They wanted to recruit drivers. They put a spin on it like each driver being an owner or something. I don't know. It's all a play on words, really."

"Oh."

"Yeah." I take another deep breath and elaborate, because I know it's what he wants to hear. Maybe then he'll understand. Maybe it'll help *me* understand more, too. "I went to his table to talk to him about his rates. I thought I could go with a smaller delivery service for food and save some money."

"I take it he wasn't any help."

"No. And I basically got laughed away from the table."

"Ouch."

"Yeah, it was kind of humiliating. But then Malcolm found me later when I was heading up to my hotel room. He apologized, invited me to dinner on him to make up for it, and I guess the rest is history. He made me laugh and he kept telling me how smart I must be to be opening a business so young. I thought he was really attractive and he was obviously flirting with me."

"Is that the first time you slept with him?" Tyler's voice is nearly a whisper.

I close my eyes. "Yeah. I didn't realize he was married at the time. Didn't pay attention to what hand his ring was on. I just thought—well, I didn't think, really. That was the issue."

"When did you find out?"

"The last day of the conference, he got a call while we were, uh…"

"Oh."

"Yeah. He told me about her and how he wasn't happy. Said he could picture himself with someone like me."

"A man?"

"I think he meant personality."

"Oh."

"Yeah."

"And you kept seeing him?" he asks.

"No, I was pissed. I told him it was over and that I didn't want to be the one he cheated on his wife with."

"So what changed?"

"A week later, he came to my house and convinced me to give him a second chance. He seemed really upset that I ignored him for a week and I felt kind of guilty—"

"For what?"

I shrug. "I guess not hearing him out. I know. It's stupid. Anyway, one thing led to another and then we were in my bedroom. He was gone in the morning but left me a note that he'd be back. That's kind of how it all started."

"How'd he know where you lived?"

"I gave him my information for delivery quotes that first day."

"Oh."

"Yeah. Anyway, after he came over, I thought he had told his wife about the affair, but it turns out he didn't. He promised me he would, though." I scoff. "He's been saying that basically every night since then."

"How long's it been?"

"Just about six months."

"Oh."

"Yeah. You probably think I'm an idiot because I love him."

"Are you sure you do?" Bold words, but I know he's just trying to make sure I'm not in a bad situation. Trouble is, I'm not that sure myself.

"I guess so. Do you ever *really* know what someone else is thinking?" I ask.

"I think you should when it comes to something like that," he says.

"Yeah, maybe."

"Who said it first?"

"He did. I was complaining about him going back to his wife—which is totally unfair of me because she's his *wife*—and we got into this huge argument. We both said some things that we probably shouldn't have. Anyway, when he apologized for what he said, he told me that he loved me."

"As an apology?"

I shrug again. "Kind of. Maybe. I don't know. I was thrown off at first, but the longer I didn't say anything, the more I could see how disappointed he was, so I said it back. Now it's just kind of automatic. I can't really take it back, can I?"

"Of course you can. Adrian, you can change your mind about anything."

I don't respond. Tyler's right. I know that. I just hate knowing I'm the one who is causing Malcolm any pain. Even if I'm *in love* with him, I *do* care about him. I don't want to hurt him.

"Do you believe him when he says he loves you?" he asks.

I suck in a shuddering breath. Tyler's really digging in deep with me tonight. I guess I don't really mind it. I want to be able to tell him more about myself. I want him to understand.

I don't answer, so he turns to me and adds, "You know he's not treating you as well as he should be. You're…you're amazing. You have so much going for you. You're fun, smart, driven."

I scoff. "I think driven is a stretch. I laid around all morning until I had to go to work."

"Adrian, you own a house and you started a very successful business. Yes, you're driven. I'm impressed."

That makes me smile.

"Has Malcolm ever told you he's proud of you?"

There goes my smile.

"He should. He should want to spend every second with you," Tyler adds. "He shouldn't be looking for excuses to avoid you."

"He's not avoiding me. He loves me."

"If he loved you, he—" But Tyler doesn't finish.

Instead, he looks back up at the sky with his mouth shut. After a minute, he adds quietly, "I wouldn't ever look for reasons to avoid you."

My heart rate quickens. What is he saying? This is weird. But a good weird. It's still weird, though. I don't know what to say—don't really even know what to think—so I just ignore it completely.

"Something needs to change with me and Malcolm, though," I admit. "I'm tired of having to hide our relationship all the time. Last night I just wanted to hold his hand and sit with him on the beach, but he wanted to go back to my house and…you know. Again."

"He doesn't…*force* you or anything, does he?"

"Not really. I mean, he sometimes has to, like, *convince* me a bit, but he always waits until I say yes."

Tyler shakes his head. "That's the same thing."

"Convince is the wrong word. I shouldn't have said that."

"But you meant it."

I ignore him. "It's not all sex. We talk and stuff…but it's still *mostly* sex."

"So how do you know you love him?"

"Because I love being with him."

Tyler turns and waits for me to look at him before continuing. "But that alone does not mean you love him. Does he know what you were like as a kid? Does he know what you want to be like when you're older? Does he judge you based on where you've been or what you've done? Does he even know what your parents do for a living? Where they live? Does he care?"

I face the sea of stars above us, but don't answer any of his questions. I can't answer them because I don't know. It scares me.

He leans up on his arm and peers over me. "I think you deserve so much better than Malcolm. Someone who cares about who you were then, who you are now, and someone who just wants to be with you no matter what you're doing. Someone who would be content just holding your hand while you watch the waves…or look at the stars. Someone who will take care of you when you're sick. Someone who is one hundred percent committed to you."

Absently, I lick my lips and a moment later, I feel his on mine. It only lasts a second, but it's enough to make my chest burn and my heart race again. My skin prickles with goosebumps and I feel as though I could be sucked up into oblivion and not even feel a thing.

When I open my eyes, he's standing with his hand out toward me.

"Come on, I want to do something," he says.

I don't think I can go any further with him. Not because it's him—that kiss was incredible—but because

I don't want to be a cheater. Just because Malcolm is doesn't mean I should be.

"Tyler, I don't think we should—it was just one kiss and—"

"No, not that," he says. "Just trust me one more time, okay?"

I take his hand and we get to our feet in the grass. He puts his arms around my waist and pulls me close. His free hand links with mine and soon we're swaying as if we're dancing.

"What are we doing?" I mutter over his shoulder.

"This is what it's like to really care for someone," he says.

"Tyler, this is—"

"Shh…just listen."

"To what?" I ask, but after a little while I hear it. The crickets, water rushing in a nearby stream, the pounding of my heartbeat. Almost like music.

I nuzzle closer to him and we move slowly, holding each other and dancing in the empty field like nothing else matters.

Tyler's right. I've never been with someone like this.

Chapter Eight:
TYLER

Mom's watching some cop show as I type away at my phone, craning in an awkward position thanks to the short cord length of the charger.

Even though it's my night off, I'd much rather be working. At least that way I could spend some time with Adrian instead of resorting to draining my phone battery texting him back and forth. Short of actually going down to the Nine and chatting him up while he tends bar in my absence, this is the closest I can be to him.

Last night was amazing. And terrifying. Exciting, but nerve-wracking. Adrian and I didn't say much as we danced under the stars. Nor did we say much on the way home. He did, however, thank me and hug me again when we got home. I texted him as soon as I got up and except for the hour that I went to his place to have lunch, we haven't stopped texting since.

There's a constant burning warmth in my belly that occasionally spreads up to my chest every time I get a reply from Adrian. It's been there since last night. It's the most uncomfortable, yet amazing feeling I've ever felt. I think Adrian feels the same way, too, because he's given me no indication otherwise. Actually, he's the one who texted me first after lunch.

It's really slow tonight, he says.

Not much going on here, either, I write back.

I'm so tired lol

Late night last night?

GREAT night last night.

That makes me smile. *Aw haha. Glad you enjoyed it*

You didn't?

Of course I did. I'm just glad you're acting like yourself again

Yeah

Is the boss going to yell at you for texting on the job?

"Who are you talking to that you're smiling so much at your phone?" Mom asks.

I look up and notice that her show has taken a commercial break. I wonder how long she's been watching me.

"Oh." I wrack my brain trying to find an excuse.

"It's, uh, Adrian. He just asked me where I put something at work."

"Okay." She doesn't seem to buy it.

"He's bored, too," I add. "Because it's so slow." My phone buzzes with a new text.

Mom turns back to the TV. "Well, tell him I said hi."

"I will. Do you need anything?" I ask. "I can get you a glass of water or reheat what's left of your dinner." She didn't eat much. Less and less each day.

"I'm fine. Shh," she shushes me now that her show is back on.

Adrian and I keep texting back and forth until it's closing time and I've long since put Mom to bed—meaning that I pulled out her evening meds and a tall glass of water and turned out the light in the living room. I'm now lying in my small bedroom that's the size of a closet with the bedside lamp on, waiting until Adrian says he's leaving.

Ugh, aren't you done yet? ;)

Just counting out the deposit

Who else is closing?

Jessica. She's slow haha

Not as good as me? I write.

Oh, NEVER. You're SUCH a pro lol

Yeah yeah yeah. I'm getting tired, so you should finish up soon

Summer Nights

You can go to bed if you want, he writes back.

But I want to see you

A few minutes pass and then he responds: *Tonight?*

Yeah

Another minute. *Oh*

What?

Malcolm's coming over…

The elated feeling that's been burning in my chest all night suddenly turns to embarrassment and drops to my stomach. Why did I think that after one night he would break up with Malcolm? I only gave him a quick peck last night. Malcolm's been giving him so much more. Physically, at least. I thought I made it clear that sex isn't the only important thing in a relationship. I thought Adrian enjoyed dancing under the stars. Now I'm afraid he thinks it was super cheesy.

I toss my phone on the nightstand, click off the lamp, and roll over in an attempt to get to sleep. I half expect to be woken up by a text from Adrian at any moment—maybe even a phone call—but my phone sits silent all night.

"What are you so grumpy about?" Bailey asks me the next morning while I'm eating breakfast. She's scouring the refrigerator for something to eat.

"Nothing," I murmur. I can't believe Adrian hasn't texted me back or anything. Does he not realize how much he was leading me on? He should've told me right from the start that he wanted to stay with Malcolm. Maybe that's why he didn't kiss me back.

"Mom said you seemed giddy last night. What changed?"

"Just leave it alone, Bailey!"

She rolls her eyes and shuts the fridge door hard and escapes into the bathroom.

By the time I'm rinsing off my bowl in the sink, she emerges again.

"Hey, I'm sorry," I say. "I'm just not having a good morning."

She softens her look. "We're having a lot of those lately."

I glance into the living room in Mom's direction. "Yeah. I want to apologize for the other day as well. I never should've pushed you. I can take care of all the finances if you're not up to it. I just didn't want to exclude you."

Bailey breathes in a deep breath. "Thanks for that.

And I'm sorry, too. For what I said. I just don't want to think about losing her. I know it's coming, but…"

I nod. "Yeah, I know."

She pushes her hair out of her face. "Anyway, if you want to talk about anything, just let me know."

"Okay. Same goes for you, though."

She smiles. "Deal."

I try to go through my day without thinking about Adrian's sudden radio-silence, but it haunts me wherever I go. I keep thinking my phone's gone off when it hasn't. Keep rereading the end of our conversation, debating on whether I was too curt or if I should text him and apologize. But what exactly would I apologize for?

I take the long way on my run so I don't have to pass by his house. I wonder if he even sees me in the thirty seconds it takes to walk from the front door to the street. A part of me hopes he does so that he thinks that none of this is really bothering me.

Maybe if I pretend that the other night didn't happen I'll feel better about being completely rejected. I doubt it, though. I take my time getting ready for work, hoping that the moment won't actually come. Yesterday I wished I was working, today I'm dreading it. I can't escape him here.

"Hey," he says when I come into the office to clock in.

I nod, but don't say anything and hurry out of the room as quickly as I can. I busy myself with cleaning every nook and cranny I can find. Pulling out drawers, mats, anything so I can clean under them. Some of these things probably haven't been touched since we opened.

"New specials tonight." Adrian carries over his pad of paper and plops it on the bar. He grabs a sponge and washes up the chalkboard.

"I'll look later." I brush by him and disappear into the kitchen. There has to be something for me to do in here before we open. Frankie's pretty much cleaned everything, though.

A few minutes later, Adrian meets me in the kitchen. "Are you okay?"

I wipe up the already-clean counters and don't look at him. "What do you think?"

"I think you're acting really weird."

"And why do you think that is, Adrian?"

"I don't know, that's why I asked!"

"Maybe we're just not as close as I thought." I walk out of the room.

Chapter Nine:
ADRIAN

"Hey, what's up?" I say into the phone when Jessie calls. I just got into the office and there's no one here yet. I figured it was the perfect opportunity to pay this month's bills. The joys of being a business owner.

"Well, I have a proposition for you," she says.

"What is it?"

"I know you couldn't legally give me alcohol to serve at the Manor for our Fourth of July party, but I was wondering if you would be interested in hosting our next fundraising event."

I prop the phone between my shoulder and my ear as I tear into an envelope. "What did you have in mind?"

"Well, the Manor isn't really built for a large party

like that. Besides, my grandma would lose it if there were that many people inside. And I figured more people would come if there was alcohol."

"So you want to have it here?"

"Yeah. Maybe have a small cover charge or something to get some extra money for us," she says. "We'd advertise it as best we can."

"Well, we can help advertise it, too." I glance over at the calendar. "When were you thinking of doing this?"

"Soon. Like…next weekend?"

"Jessie, that's crazy!"

"I know!" I can picture her cringing on the other side. "I know it is, but we're not doing so well over here and I'd really appreciate it. Besides, I noticed that you guys never came to our Fourth of July party and this would be a good way to make up for it."

Guilt trip. I was waiting to see when she'd pull that on me.

"Okay," I say with a sigh. "We'll make it work. Saturday's are usually our busiest nights, so we'll just dedicate the whole night to it. You can have your cover charge and then we'll split the profit from alcohol fifty-fifty. We'll keep the profit from food. Does that work?"

"Actually, Marsha at the diner is donating some burgers that we were hoping to sell off too."

I tap my pen on the desk as I consider this.

"Uh…okay. How about you sell those on the patio, but we'll still have food from the bar available inside, so we can still make a profit from that too. That way, once the burgers are gone, people will order more from our menu."

"Are you sure that's okay?"

"Yeah, it'll be fine," I say. "Is there anything else we need to think of? Decorations, fliers, anything?"

"Grandma is insisting on having a Chinese auction. I think it won't be that kind of party, but she wants it."

"Okay, we can make room for that. Just have people write their phone numbers on the back because the likelihood of them holding onto their tickets in a bar are slim."

She chuckles on the other end. "True."

"We'll make it work."

"Thank you so much, Adrian!"

The happiness in her voice makes me smile. "You're welcome. We'll need all the help we can get, though. That means you, your grandma, even Mason if he wants."

"Oh, Robyn told you about him, huh?"

"He stopped in the bar one night. Tyler met him and figured it together. It was actually the night that you, uh…"

She clears her throat. "Yeah. Not my finest hour."

"We all have them. So we can count on three people?"

"Uh, no. Just me and Grandma. Mason's not—Mason went home."

"Oh." Wow. Open mouth, insert foot. "I'm sorry."

"It's fine. Thanks for your help. You can email me some of the details or I could stop by sometime if you want."

"Yeah, I'll give you a call probably tomorrow once I've had a chance to think get it all down on paper."

"Thanks again."

"No problem."

When the call ends, Tyler walks in to punch in for the day. I look up and offer a tight smile, but he doesn't even glance in my direction. The next moment, he's out of the room.

He made it very clear last week that he didn't want to talk to me, so I've been giving him space. And he's been doing his work and being just as friendly with the customers, so I can't really say much about him giving me the silent treatment at work. I just don't like it.

I know he's upset with me for staying with Malcolm, but what am I supposed to do? Dump my boyfriend because of one kiss? Okay, sure, it might have only been one kiss *physically*, but it was more than that. I know it was. The connection we shared was unlike any

I've ever felt with anyone else. Not even Malcolm. Things have always been different when it comes to Tyler. That night in the field, though, that was different even for us.

Maybe that's what's been keeping me away from Tyler this week too. I'm afraid to admit it to myself. How long have I had these feelings for him? Just since that night in the field? Longer? Forever? Seeing Tyler every day mixed with whatever I'm feeling seems like a betrayal of Malcolm's trust. I don't want to hurt him.

I do my best not talk to Tyler the rest of the day. If space is what he wants, space is what he'll get. He'll come to me when he's ready. We'll work it out. I hope.

"Hey, can you bring that order of cocktails over to Table Three?" I ask him when I come to the bar to grab a round of beers for Table Six. "Carrie's swamped and they've already been waiting for twenty minutes."

Tyler doesn't say anything, but grabs the tray and carries them over to the correct table, passing them out with a smile.

I fill the glasses, toss out more beer with the foam than I anticipate and hastily bring them over to Table Six. If Tyler doesn't want to even acknowledge me, I won't acknowledge him.

It's petty, I know. But right now I'm feeling pretty small with the way he's been acting around me. The only solace for tonight is that I'll get to go home to Malcolm.

As the night wears on, it's painfully obvious that Tyler and I are no longer talking once the music stops and we're both quietly sweeping our corners of the restaurant. I can hear Carrie and Frankie murmuring to each other in the kitchen. Maybe they're not talking about us, but it feels like they are.

Tyler doesn't wait for me to close up the business end of things in the office before he leaves. Not that I'm surprised. On the lonely walk home in the dark, I continue to replay the events of tonight in my head. Rather, the *lack* of events. How can silence cause so much tension in my shoulders? Maybe I can ask Malcolm to rub them later.

Back at my house, Malcolm clicks off the TV when I step through the door.

"Hey, babe, how was work?"

I shrug and kick off my shoes by the door. "Just all right."

"Slow night?"

"No, actually it was really busy." I take a seat next to him on the couch.

"That's good. Bet you made a lot of money."

"Huh? Oh yeah, we did." I don't even remember how much the deposit was for. Good thing I wrote it down. "Can you rub my back?"

He smiles. "Of course, babe. Come on, lay down in the bed. It'll be easier."

I follow him to my room and pull off my shirt before lying on my stomach on the bed. Malcolm comes behind me and soon I feel his rough hands on my shoulders.

"Do you ever think about the future?" My eyes are closed and my face is mostly smushed against the pillows, but Malcolm's hands working the knots out of my back feels so good.

"What do you mean?"

"Like you and me. Where we'll be in five, ten years?"

"Well, I'll definitely be divorced by then. It'll just be me and you. And we can do this anytime you want." His hands move lower down my back and I reach around.

"No, my shoulders. Do my shoulders."

He sighs heavily, but moves his hands back up to where they were.

"I meant, do you think we'll get married? Have kids?"

Malcolm scoffs. "I don't think so. I've done the marriage thing and look how that turned out. Besides, I'm getting a little old for kids."

My heart sinks a bit. I thought that's what we were

working toward? "I'm not too old."

He leans forward and kisses my ear. "I know, babe, but I don't really want kids. I just want it to be me and you."

"What about a dog?"

"We're not home enough for a dog," he says.

It's as if everything I thought I knew about our relationship has been wiped away. What I believed to be true last week is no longer true now. I thought Tyler was my best friend, but after one weird evening, I'm thinking he might mean more to me. All the while his actions show that he cares *less* about me. Meanwhile, I thought Malcolm and I were working toward a future together that would evolve beyond these evening meet-ups and now it seems like he's content with our arrangement remaining the status quo.

My world is spinning and I don't know how to stop it.

Malcolm rolls next to me. "You're quiet."

"Just thinking."

"Uh oh." He laughs. "About what? The dog?"

"No, not—" I hesitate. I know I need to tell Malcolm about kissing Tyler. I would want to know if it were reversed. But what's the easiest way to say it? And how do I tell him something like that without giving away what I'm feeling? I don't want Malcolm to think

I'm leaving him. I love him, don't I?

He wraps his arms around me and pulls me close. "Babe, what is it?"

I breathe in a deep breath. "You have to promise not to get mad."

"I can't promise that if I don't know what it is yet."

"I guess that's true." I pick at a thread in the bedspread. "You remember those two nights we were supposed to spend together, but you had to stay home the second night? It was around the Fourth of July."

"Yeah…" he says slowly.

"That was — I was really upset by that."

"I'm sorry, babe." He kisses my shoulder.

"And Tyler noticed that I was upset and suggested we hang out after work."

He narrows his eyes. "Okay."

"So we went to this old farm field outside of town and watched the stars and talked and — " Pressure builds in my chest. " — he kissed me."

Malcolm pulls away from me and sits up. "He *what*?"

I sit up too. "It was just a quick kiss. And it was only once!"

"And did you tell him to get lost?"

I swallow hard and my voice drops to nearly a whisper. "No."

"Did you like it?"

"Malcolm, come on, I don't want to do this with you," I say, avoiding the question. "I just wanted to be honest with you. We can be honest with each other, can't we?"

He puts his hands on his hips and chews on the inside of his cheek as he studies me. Finally, he grunts and says, "Yeah, we can be honest with each other. So tell me this, is that the only time something like this has happened?"

"Yes," I say quickly, nodding my head for effect. "Just once."

"And have you talked to him since it happened?"

"Not really," I say honestly.

"Good. Let's keep it that way."

Chapter Ten:
TYLER

Tonight's the night of the fundraiser for Montana Manor at the Nine, so it's all hands on deck. I came in early to help, but also because I couldn't stand to sit at home *thinking* anymore.

I shuffle around, making sure we're all stocked up on alcohol and everything's as clean as it can get before people start showing up.

I try to avoid talking to Adrian as much as I can like I've been doing the past two weeks. I know it's been a while, but I'm still mad at him for seeing Malcolm again. Mostly, I'm mad at him for leading me on. Funny how the texts just dropped off completely as soon as Malcolm was ready to spend time with him. Guess I'm only good enough as a substitute.

"Oh, Tyler, dear," Ethel calls to me when I come out of the stock room for what feels like the millionth time today. She's Jessie's grandmother and co-owner of Montana Manor.

"Hmm?"

"Oh, look at you. Always so handsome," she pats my cheek and smiles.

I can't help but grin like an idiot. "Thanks."

"I have quite a big favor to ask of you, if you wouldn't mind."

"Uh, sure, what is it?"

"We've had a young man staying with us for most of the summer," she starts.

"Mason? I actually met him once."

She claps her hands together and beams. "Oh good! Well, he has decided to stay with us a bit longer, but Jessie doesn't know it yet. He wants to surprise her tonight. Would you mind finding a place for him to hide out until he's ready?"

"Uh..." I look around and try to determine the best place for him. "Yeah, sure. I'll find someplace. When's he coming?"

"Well, he's going to wait until I call to tell him Jessie's busy," she explains. "So I'll have to think of something to distract her while he sneaks in."

I nod. "Got it. Just let me know when he's on his way."

She smiles. "Thank you, dear. You're so wonderful."

Even though I know Ethel's nice to everyone, it still cheers me up.

When I return to the bar to finish unloading, Adrian comes out of the kitchen and steps behind the bar before I can sneak away. We look at each other, both of us clearly wanting to say something, but neither of us having the courage to actually say it.

"Hey," he says.

"Hey." I divert my eyes and step around him, but he catches my arm.

"Uh, can we talk sometime?"

I pull my arm free. "I'm kind of busy right now."

This is the first time in two weeks that he's said anything to me that's not work-related. What's changed? Nothing on my end. He's still a jerk and I'm not ready to forgive him for blowing me off after I put myself out there.

Especially not tonight.

For the next hour, I zigzag across from stock room to bar to kitchen, looking for things to busy myself with. I set up the tables for the Chinese auction in the corner. I reorganize the bottles in the back. I even sweep under the freezer behind the bar.

Finally, Ethel waves me over to the front door. She

grabs my shoulder to pull me down so she can whisper in my ear.

"I just asked Jessie to help unload the firewood. Mason will be here any minute. I'll make sure she's not looking in here so you can sneak him in."

I nod. "Okay."

Five minutes later, with Jessie distracted by the firewood, Mason slowly creeps through the door and peers inside.

I step over and shake his hand. "Mason, hi. I hear you're looking for a place to hide?"

He laughs. "I guess that's the plan."

I lead him to the stock room. "Well, this is the best I've got, unless you want to chill in the freezer." I nudge him and chuckle to myself. "Get it? *Chill.*"

He rolls his eyes with a grin. "That was dumb."

"Anyway, I guess you're just going to hang out here until you're ready to make your entrance. At least, that's what I got from Ethel."

He nods. "Yup. I've got it all planned out."

"Okay, well, let me know if you need anything."

"I will, thanks," he says.

When I come through the door to get back to work, Adrian nearly crashes into me.

"Oh, sorry!" he says, then smiles wide.

I try not to look bothered by his presence and hook

my thumb over my shoulder. "Mason's hiding out to surprise Jessie later, so keep it quiet."

"Okay." He grabs my arm when I turn to leave. "Hey, when can we get a moment to talk?"

A part of me wants to hear him out. A *big* part of me. I just want to talk to him—not about our *feelings* or that kiss or any of that. I just want to talk to him about…anything. Like we used to.

But I'm still mad at him. And I want him to know that.

I point out to the beach. "Jessie asked me to help man the fire all night, so I should go help."

He releases me. "Oh. Right, yeah. That's important."

I nod. "Yeah."

Another moment passes where we just look at each other. I wonder what he's thinking—why he wants to talk all of a sudden—but instead I turn and head out to the beach.

Two hours later, the sun has begun to set, the fire is roaring, and the crowd from inside the bar has spilled out to the beach. Several people circle the fire with drinks, laughing and talking.

After I toss another log onto the fire, I look back inside, hoping Adrian's looking out here. I hope he's torn up, wondering if I'm thinking of him, whether I'm still mad, going back and forth about where we stand. But every time I look up toward the bar where he's pouring drinks and laughing with customers, he's not looking this way.

I plop in the sand and stare at the fire. How could one kiss—that lasted only a fraction of a second—change so much? But then, I know it's been more than just that kiss.

I've realized these last few weeks just how much I like him. Those feelings didn't just come up overnight. They've been building for a long time. But since he was taken I didn't say anything. And nobody knew that I was even interested in another guy—*I* barely knew. It was better not to say anything and have to go through the whole *coming out* thing if it was just a crush.

But meeting Malcolm and hearing about the way he treats Adrian changed things. I'm more protective of him than I thought. I want him to be mine so that nobody can hurt him. So that I can be everything he deserves.

I just don't know if he likes me too. The night we danced under the stars I thought he did, but he hasn't talked to me much since then. Now all of a sudden he wants to? I don't know. This whole situation sucks.

Another look up at the bar and I see Jessie and Mason walking out hand-in-hand. They stop on the patio and kiss, breaking for a moment to talk to each other.

Finally, they come down to the sand and take a seat on the other side of the fire, wrapped in each other's arms. I'm glad they're happy, but it's a little surprising after she slapped him a few weeks ago. They must've worked out a lot of stuff.

I wonder if Adrian and I can work it out, too. Today it seems like he's been trying to. Maybe I've stewed enough and now it's time to grow up and hear him out.

That's probably what I should do. I have to watch the fire the rest of the night, but I'll talk to him when we close. Like we usually do.

As the night wears on, the crowd slowly starts to die down. I feed fewer logs to the fire and soon there's only three other people outside besides Jessie, Mason, and myself. I look and see that Adrian's still inside behind the bar, wiping up the counter and pocketing some of his tip money. There are two people chatting and laughing with drinks in their hands.

I look out along the beach and see Malcolm approaching. I groan. I was hoping to have some alone time with Adrian now that I've decided to talk to him.

Malcolm trudges through the sand in black work boots and his T-shirt tucked into his jeans. He definitely seems out of place for a beach party. He looks right at me as he comes closer. I slowly get to my feet. He grabs my arm and pulls me toward the Pier, away from the safety of the firelight.

"I want to talk to you," he mutters.

My feet scramble to keep up with him as he pulls me along. We march on into the darkness until he releases me under the Pier.

He puts his hands on his hips and sets his jaw.

"Who do you think you are?" he snarls.

"What are you talking about?"

"You know what I'm talking about! You think you're just going to sweep in and take him away from me?"

"Adrian? I think he can make his own decisions." I cross my arms and try to not look intimidated. *Try.* I wish we were closer to the Nine. Closer to lights. Closer to people.

He jabs his finger in my chest. "You're hoping that he'll decide to be with you."

How much did Adrian tell him?

"I don't think that's what he wants," I say.

"So you just decided to kiss him, even if he's taken?"

"I didn't kiss him to *win* him. I kissed him because I care about him."

"Well, he's off limits!" He turns and takes a step back toward the Nine as if the matter is settled.

I hate the power he thinks he has over Adrian. If Malcolm is being this controlling and demanding with me, I can only imagine what he's like when he's alone with Adrian.

"Oh, so it's okay for you to sleep with someone else, but not for him?" I shout at him. "Sounds pretty hypocritical to me."

He spins around. I don't see his fist until it's right in front of me. Too late.

I fall back in the sand as heat surges to my cheek and it starts to throb.

"Hey!" Mason calls from behind Malcolm. He jogs over to us.

"Tyler, are you okay?" Jessie shouts, trailing Mason.

They're both at my side within seconds. Jessie pulls my hand away from my cheek and grabs my shoulders to look at me. Mason stands and looks back toward the Nine.

"That guy didn't look friendly, so we followed," Jessie says. She makes a face when she sees mine and looks up at Mason. "We need to get him some ice."

"Are you okay to walk?" Mason asks me.

There's no way I'm going to let him carry me after I just got sucker-punched. I get to my feet on my own, but still Jessie and Mason grab my arms to help steady me.

"What happened?" Jessie asks. Her arm is hooked around me, although it's unnecessary. It's still nice to know she's there for me. "Who was that guy?"

"Nothing. He's no one." It's too long—and embarrassing—of a story.

"He has to be *someone*," she pushes. "Why else would he punch you?"

We get inside the Nine. Luckily most of the customers have left for the night, except the two at the bar. Adrian's nowhere to be seen, though.

Mason and Jessie lead me to the office where she rushes to pull the ice pack out of the freezer.

"What's going on?" Ethel asks breathlessly, stepping into the small, crowded room. "Should I call the police?"

"No, Grandma, he's okay," Jessie says as she pushes the ice pack against my face. She looks at me. "Unless you want to press charges?"

What I want is to not have all this attention. But that's something I'm not going to get.

I shake my head. "No, I don't. Where's Adrian?"

"He left with an older man who came in from the beach," Ethel says. "Didn't say hi to anyone. I don't really think that boy wanted to go with him."

I slump in my seat, doing my best to fight the tears. "Oh no."

Why did I have to rub it in that Malcolm's a hypocrite? He never would've punched me and he might've just *left*. Now he's with Adrian after I pissed him off. God only knows what's going on.

"What? What is it?" Ethel asks.

I cover my face with my free hand and don't say anything.

"Can you guys give us a minute?" Jessie asks, looking between Ethel and Mason.

He takes the hint and says, "Come on, Ethel, we can start cleaning up."

When they're gone, Jessie shuts the door and sits on the desk.

"You have to call Adrian," I tell her. "Get someone to his house. He could be—I don't think he's safe." I search for my phone, but can't find it. I must've dropped it in the sand somewhere.

"Why? What are you talking about? Tyler, what's going on?" she asks.

I let out a heavy sigh. "That was Malcolm. Adrian's…boyfriend."

"Ooooh," she says slowly. "And you think he's going to hurt Adrian?"

"He just hit me!"

She types on her phone—hopefully to Adrian— and says, "True."

"He's not right for Adrian. I tried to tell him that and I thought he listened, but he's still with Malcolm and now they're alone and he's pissed—"

"Wait, slow down," Jessie says. "Is Malcolm the secret man-friend? Adrian hasn't said much about him."

"He's keeping him a secret…because he's married."

"He's *what*? To a woman?"

I nod and readjust the ice pack on my face.

"How did that even get started?"

"It's a long story, but he's just using Adrian. I tried to convince him. I even—" Nope, not going there. She doesn't need to know that. "I'm just really worried about him. He deserves so much better than that. Malcolm just wants to control him."

Jessie's quiet for a while as she digests it all. I try not to think of what's happening to Adrian now that Malcolm's pissed off. Is he going to punch him too? More? Will Adrian be okay without a crowd?

Why hasn't Adrian responded to Jessie's text?

"Tyler," she says quietly. "Are you and Adrian…?"

I swallow the lump in my throat. "It was just a kiss. Just a peck, really. We didn't—I wasn't trying to make things worse. I just wanted…I don't know."

She takes my hand and squeezes. "Okay. It'll all be okay."

"How? Where's Adrian now? How do we know

Malcolm's not hitting him, too?"

"I texted him. If Malcolm's his boyfriend, I don't think he'll hurt him. But we'll call him if we have to. When we get you home, we'll stop at his house if he hasn't answered us by then. Adrian will be okay. We have to make sure *you're* okay too, though."

I shake my head. "I'm still worried about him. Even if he doesn't want to be with me, he shouldn't be with someone like that. He deserves better."

Chapter Eleven:
ADRIAN

Malcolm and I walk in silence back to my house. He's not in the mood. I knew that the moment he came into the Nine from the beach and nearly dragged me out of there. It was embarrassing. There were still a couple customers there. I didn't do any of the closing stuff. At least Ethel saw me leave, so hopefully she can relay to everyone else that I didn't just ditch.

Malcolm didn't really give me a chance to protest. The fact that he was even at the Nine at all startled me. To my knowledge, the only time he's been there was when he met Tyler.

I wonder if he's the problem. Tyler is my co-worker and Malcolm doesn't like that. Or maybe I'm reading too much into it and Malcolm just got into a fight with his wife and wants to blow off some steam. But he should know by now that I'm serious when it comes to work.

I don't dare send a text to Tyler to ask him to close up. Malcolm would wonder who I'm texting and I know he wouldn't be happy with me keeping in touch with him.

When we get to my house, Malcolm stands behind me as I unlock the door. Almost like a parent about to scold their kid. It's the only time in our relationship that I've felt like this. Insignificant. I hate it.

I try to put distance between us by escaping into the kitchen, but he follows. I can feel the rage radiating off of him. I don't like it. I wish he would just go away right now. How did I get here?

"So you're not going to say anything?" he asks.

I flick on the light for added safety. I feel better with it on.

"Say something about what?" I keep my back to him as I fill a glass with water at the faucet.

"Your other little boyfriend," he says sarcastically. "You know, the one who works for you."

"Tyler's not my boyfriend. You are." I bite my tongue from adding an insult.

"If that were true, you wouldn't be off kissing him when I'm away."

I start putting away the dishes stacked in the rack

by the sink. Just to keep my hands busy. "That's interesting, coming from you."

"What's that supposed to mean?"

"You know what it means."

He grabs my shoulder and spins me around, pinning me against the counter. "That's different."

I push away from him and go out to the living room. "How's it different?" I flick on the lights in here too.

"I told you. I'm leaving her."

"And when is that going to happen?" I snap. My confidence has returned now that there's more space between us. "You've been saying that since we started."

He runs his tongue over his teeth. "Listen, I say it's going to happen, so it's going to happen. You just have to trust me."

"Then you should trust me, too, with what happened with Tyler," I counter. "I'm still with you, aren't I?"

"I don't know. *Are you?*"

I narrow my eyes. "What are you talking about?"

"If you really loved me, you wouldn't even entertain the idea of being with anyone else."

"Just like you're doing with your wife?"

"That's different. She was with me first."

"That didn't stop you from sleeping with me."

"Because I love you. I don't want anyone else to have you."

That really makes me angry. "Is that what you were doing at the Nine earlier? Marking your territory?"

"So what? I wanted them to know that you have to answer to me."

I pause and stare at him because I honestly don't know what to say. He doesn't know me at all if he thinks that statement is true.

"That's not—no, you're not—I don't *control* you," he says quickly.

"Funny, because that's what you said."

"No, I just meant—" He sighs and takes a step toward me, reaching for my hands. "I'm sorry."

I'm not going to let him dictate the situation like this. He can't just turn on a dime and start acting sweet when a minute ago he was accusing me of cheating on him.

I pull away and put my hands on my hips. "For what?"

"Being an ass." He gives me a sad look that— despite my best efforts—threatens to break down my wall of anger. It makes me mad at myself for being weak enough to fall for something like that.

"About?" He's not going to get out of this easily, that's for sure.

"Tyler."

"And?"

Another sigh. "What do you want me to say?"

"I want you to apologize for embarrassing me like that at work," I say. "*I'm* the boss there. I can't be running off before closing without any notice to my employees. One of them just *happens* to be Tyler."

Malcolm steps back and shakes his head. "I don't like you two seeing each other knowing you've had history."

"History? It was just—" I stop myself from saying, *It was just one kiss*. It was so much more than that. It meant something to me. I suspect it meant something to Tyler, too. I don't want to downplay it and steal from its meaning.

But I made a commitment to Malcolm. I have to honor that.

"Just what?" he presses.

I look away. "Just drop it."

"You have feelings for him, don't you?" His voice raises again.

I stare at the floor, refusing to answer him. At this point, I'm only with Malcolm out of loyalty—and guilt for ruining his marriage—but is that reason enough to stay with him?

My head snaps up at the sound of a crash.

Malcolm's holding what's left of the back of one of the kitchen chairs. The rest if smashed on the floor in the doorway. He stares at me through heavy breaths.

My heart races and I mentally plan my route in case I need to escape.

I *should* escape.

"I put my marriage on the line for you!" he bellows.

"You put your marriage on the line for some ass," I shoot back.

He ignores me. "And now you've found someone else?"

I don't want to entertain his paranoia. "You have absolutely no intention of leaving your wife, do you? I mean, why would you when you have the best of both worlds? Loving wife at home, eager lover on the side, right?"

That got his attention. "Shut your mouth."

"No, I think it's time I hear the truth," I push. "You aren't going to leave your wife, are you? All these promises you've been making with me are empty, aren't they? You like this arrangement because you're the only one benefitting from it."

He doesn't say anything. For a long time.

Finally, I give up and go to my room, slamming the door behind me. If Malcolm wanted to keep fighting, he would've said something. Maybe I'll get lucky and he'll take the hint and leave. I don't think that's going to happen, though.

There's a text waiting for me from Jessie from twenty minutes ago. *Are you okay?*

Yeah, I'm fine. Sorry for leaving early. Something came up, I write back.

I text Tyler to apologize for leaving early, but I don't expect an answer back. He didn't want to talk all day, so why would it be any different now? Especially since it looks like I ditched.

Five minutes pass without a response from Tyler or Jessie, so I decide to go back out and see what Malcolm's doing. Maybe he's cooled down enough that we can have a civilized conversation.

He's sitting in the doorway between the kitchen and the living room trying to piece the chair he broke back together.

I walk up and lean on the wall with my arms crossed. He doesn't look up.

"Hey," I say.

"Are you sure you want to talk to me after what we both said?"

I sigh. "I'm sorry about that. And I'm sorry you feel threatened. I just wanted to be honest with you about the kiss. That's why I told you right away."

"I still don't like it."

I pause and consider the best way to address it without my resentment to his marriage coming through. "Tyler's my friend. I'm not just going to stop talking to him because he has feelings for me."

"Are you saying you don't have feelings for him?"

"I'm saying you have nothing to worry about."

"So you do?"

I kneel down beside him and catch his eye. "Whenever you go back home, I'm afraid that you're going to decide that maintaining your marriage is more important than us."

"But I love you."

I'm about to say that I love him too, but I realize it's more of a reflex. What else do you say to someone who tells you they love you other than that you feel the same way? Even when you don't?

Instead, I deflect. "It's not always that simple, though."

Malcolm reaches for me and pulls me toward him for a kiss. It's nice. It's comfortable. That's it.

"I'll go tell her right now if you want," he says.

How long have I been waiting for him to say that? How long have I been hoping that sharing him would come to an end? Now that he's saying it—and might actually mean it—it doesn't feel right. If he ever truly meant it, it wouldn't have taken him this long to say it.

"It's not the same if *you* don't want it, too," I tell him.

"I do." He kisses me again, getting to his knees so he's at the same level as me. He leans into me more. "I love you." He kisses across my cheek to my jaw and down my neck.

I know where this is going.

I can't help but think of Tyler and our kiss. That was so innocent. So genuine with no other meaning behind it other than affection. Kissing with Malcolm has always been purposeful. Lustful. Almost empty, even. Like he would be enjoying it just as much if it were with anyone else.

Tyler kissed me because it was *me*. And that was it. One simple kiss that's stuck in my mind ever since. He showed me something new. Not something I know deep down doesn't work.

I pull away from Malcolm. "Stop."

"What?"

"What are you doing?"

"Just trying to show you how much I love you," he says. "Just like I always have." He works his hand under my shirt. "It's never been our issue."

I push him away and get to my feet. "Except that it's *exactly* what our issue is."

"What are you talking about, babe?" He looks

more confused than hurt.

I cross my arms to keep my hands from shaking. "I think you should leave."

Malcolm jumps up and hugs me. "What are you saying?"

I don't meet his eyes. "I don't want to keep doing this anymore. Just go home to your wife…and stay there."

"Don't do this, babe. We love each other, remember? We're going to have everything we've dreamed of. I'll go home and call it off with her right now. Just wait for me."

I shake my head. My eyes are shut tight so I can't be swayed with that look that he always tries to give me. "No. It's over, Malcolm. I want you to leave."

He squeezes me tighter. Hard. I can feel his anger start to slip through. "Adrian, come on!"

I push him away. "Go!"

He's quiet, but I refuse to open my eyes and risk him sweet-talking me. I need to stand my ground. Tyler's right. This relationship with Malcolm isn't good. I can see that now.

He clears his throat. "Uh, I guess I'll call you tomorrow or something."

I bite my bottom lip and wait until I hear the door shut before I open my eyes to an empty room.

D. Allen

It's quiet.

I sink to the floor and lay flat on my back. I stare at the ceiling as the tears pool out of my eyes. I'll miss him and I still care for him, but the overwhelming emotion I'm feeling at this moment isn't remorse or regret. It's relief.

Gone are the days of wondering when I'm going to see him again. Thinking about how much longer I have with him. Worrying that he's going to decide to stay with his wife.

I made the decision for him. And I'm okay.

Chapter Twelve:
TYLER

My loud truck silences when Bailey cuts the engine in our driveway.

"I'll get the door," she says.

"You don't have to—" The door slams and cuts me off. I watch her come around to my side and notice that nearly all the lights are on at Adrian's house. What more is that Malcolm's vehicle isn't in the driveway. I can't deny that that's a relief.

The truck door opens and Bailey reaches for my hand to help me out. It's nice that she wants to help, but I'm not crippled. Just bruised.

"What's going on?" Adrian runs toward me and Bailey from his house. "What happened? Are you okay?"

I press the warm ice pack to my face to conceal it

more and I slam the door shut behind me. Seeing him reminds me of the choice he made. Malcolm over me. I ignore him and follow Bailey to the house. Still, I'm glad that Adrian seems to be okay.

"Tyler, what's going on?" he insists.

I stop, but keep my head down. I want to know what happened when he left, but the story needs to start with what happened to me. "Your boyfriend punched me because he thought I was coming on to you."

Bailey doesn't know what happened between me and Adrian—I haven't told anyone—but at this moment, he's the only one on my mind.

"He's not my boyfriend."

I turn and look at him with the eye that isn't covered by an ice pack. I debate whether he's telling the truth. He seems to be. Still, my throbbing cheek raises the question, "Why would you tell him about that night at all?"

He asks Bailey, "Can you give us a minute?"

She looks over at me, but my attention is on Adrian.

"I'll be inside," she says softly.

When she's gone, Adrian takes a step toward me. "How's your face?"

"It's fine."

"Can I see?"

I sigh and pull the ice pack away. Adrian comes closer and tilts my head to try to get a better look. His fingertips gently touch my skin.

"Hmm, I can't really see it in this light," he says. "Come back to my place so I can really take a look at it."

I'm about to tell him no, that Bailey can take care of it just fine, but he grabs my hand to lead me and suddenly I'm lightheaded. Just like I was that night in the field.

When we get inside, the first thing I see is the smashed chair in the doorway to the kitchen. I look around for any other damage and even give Adrian a quick once-over—noting that he's still holding my hand.

"What happened?" I ask.

"Oh, um, nothing." He pulls his hand away from mine and motions to the couch. "Here, take a seat."

I sit down and remove the warm ice pack. He tilts my head up toward the light again and inspects my face.

"Well, I don't think anything's broken," he says.

Just what they determined at the bar too.

"How bad does it feel?"

I shrug. "Just puffy."

"You should probably keep icing it." He grabs the ice pack I brought over. "I'll throw this in the freezer and get you a fresh one."

I watch as he steps over the broken chair. In my

head I picture Malcolm coming after Adrian with it. Or Adrian using it as the only thing to defend himself with. I hope neither of those things are true. I hope Malcolm's never laid a hand on Adrian like that. Although, a part of me wonders if that's why Adrian broke up with him.

He comes back with a fresh ice pack. It stings my skin when I press it against my face, but I know it's helping, so I bear with it.

"Are you cold?" he asks. "Here, let me get you a blanket."

Before I can protest, he disappears into his room and comes back a moment later with his comforter.

"This will keep the rest of you warm, at least." He fans it out over me.

"What are you doing?" I ask.

"Just trying to make sure you're comfortable."

"No, I meant—never mind."

"What?"

I shrug. "Forget it."

Adrian sits next to me and fidgets with his fingernails. I stare at the broken chair, trying to piece together what happened before I came. I want to know, but I don't want to ask Adrian and show my cards.

I'm afraid, basically. It's stupid. I should be able to tell him what's on my mind. Isn't that what I decided earlier? Before Malcolm punched me, that is. I keep my mouth shut.

"Do you want to watch TV or something?" he asks after a minute.

I shake my head.

We're quiet again. The ceiling fan hums as it spins. A car passes by on the street. Meanwhile, I'm too worried about being vulnerable that I'm trapped in my own head.

"I hope you're not still mad at me." Adrian keeps his eyes on his nails as he speaks. "I mean, of course you are. I was an ass and you're the one who paid for it." He gives up on his nails and clasps his hands together. "I'm sorry. For what Malcolm did to you. For continuing to see him after we kissed. For avoiding you lately. For even dating him at all. You were right. He wasn't good for me. And now I've hurt someone I really care about. A lot."

I swallow hard. "It's okay, Adrian."

He shakes his head and looks down at the floor. "It's not, though. You saw it from the beginning. You knew that he only wanted one thing." He runs his hands over his head. "I feel so stupid for not seeing it myself."

"You were in love."

"No, I thought I was." He looks me in the eyes. "You know what I felt when I saw you through the window getting out of the truck all beaten up?"

"It was only one punch," I clarify.

"I felt like *I* had been punched right in the face." He ignores me. "For the first time I saw the pain I was causing you. I just wish it hadn't come to physical pain. I'm so sorry, Tyler."

"It's okay."

"It's not." He sinks to the floor and kneels in front of me, taking my free hand. "I broke up with Malcolm because I saw for the first time what true love was. And it wasn't what I had with him."

My heart races. I forget about my cheek for a minute and set the ice pack down. My mouth goes dry and my breath is short, but I love it.

"I've made a lot of bad decisions lately, but the one I made tonight to break things off with him—the one I thought I would never make—didn't scare me anymore. I have you. And whether that's just as a neighbor, a friend, or more, I know you'll always be there and I want to always be there for you."

I'm lost in Adrian's eyes. In his words.

"I love you, Tyler," he continues. "I think on some level I've always known. I'm just sorry it took all of this happening for me to see it. And I know I hurt you, but if you let me, I'm going to try to make up for that."

I stare at him, in shock that this is happening. I

don't know what to say, but all I know is that it makes me really happy. *He* makes me happy.

It must show, too, because his face breaks into a smile. Before he can add anything else, I pull him up closer to me and kiss him. I wrap my arms around him and squeeze tight. Now that I have him, I'm never letting him go.

His face bumps into me as we fall onto the couch together and I grunt from the pain.

"Oh, sorry."

I ignore it and continue to smile at him. We're inches away from each other. I pull the blanket over both of us, as if to shield this moment from the outside world. I want to savor it for a while.

"I love you, too," I murmur. It sounds weird to hear it out loud, but it's what I've been wanting to say since the night in the back of the truck when I first realized it myself.

Adrian smiles wide. "I love hearing you say that."

"I'll say it over and over as long as you don't ditch me for a married guy again."

His smile fades. "Yeah, I wasn't thinking straight."

I put my hand on his cheek. "Doesn't matter anymore. It's in the past. We're the future."

"You're right. And since I'm partially to blame for your recent disfigurement—"

"Um, just a bruise," I clarify, but again he ignores me.

"I think that you should stay here for a few days while I nurse you back to health."

"Oh, so jumping from one guy to the next?" I joke. "Do you ever sleep alone?"

He laughs. "Okay, I deserve that. No, this will be different. We'll take it slow."

"Moving in half an hour after your last boyfriend left? Doesn't sound slow to me." I smile at him.

"Do you want my help or not?"

"Are you sure you're not just afraid to be alone?"

He considers this. "I don't want to be alone. That's probably why I stayed with Malcolm. I just wanted to be with somebody. Anybody. But you're not just *anybody*. You're you. I want you here. And besides, you helped me enjoy the quiet before, I'm sure you can do it again."

"So you're going to help me get better and I'm going to help you?"

"That's the plan. What do you think?"

He considers for a moment. "On one condition."

"What's that?"

"I want a dog…someday."

I laugh and wrap my arms around him. "*Someday*, sure. I think I could live with that."

Behind the Book:

Summer Nights

I didn't think I'd ever write gay characters again. There are just too many assumptions made when you slap a big "gay" tag on something. I didn't want to dive into stereotypes or further enhance how gay people are different. What I wanted to do was write a story about two people falling in love, which I think I managed to do with this book.

The idea for this story first came to me when I was listening to Sugarland's song "Stay." If you're not familiar with it, it's a song about a woman who's in love with a married man. For most of the song she's begging him to stay with her until she realizes that their relationship isn't healthy and then tells him to stay with his wife.

Sound familiar?

I've been listening to that song for a while and I always thought it *had* to be told from a woman's perspective. But then I got to thinking: *What if it wasn't?* What if that same situation was told from a man's perspective? Only, in this new tale, what if the person the wife and the lover have to share is a *man*?

Well, that got my wheels turning and I set the idea aside until I had the perfect series to write it into. When it came time to plot this book, everything came easily and I felt like I already knew the story as I was writing it.

I actually got a lot of inspiration from country songs in this book and I've added a few easter eggs in it if you pay attention to them. They're mostly in the first chapter when Malcolm gets the call from his wife.

- When Adrian kneels on the bed and asks, "Why don't you stay?" – "Stay," Sugarland
- When Adrian asks Malcolm, "Don't you want to stay?" – "Don't You Wanna Stay," Jason Aldean and Kelly Clarkson
- When Adrian wonders why Malcolm's wife gets allowed to have his birthdays, holidays, and his daytimes when he only gets a few of his nights. – "Does He Love You," Reba McEntire and Linda Davis

Summer Nights

- When Adrian and Tyler dance in the field to the sound of crickets and a nearby stream. – "Heartbeat," Carrie Underwood

The title for this book came very easily and actually helped me title the other books in the series because I knew from the get-go that I wanted this book to be called *Summer Nights*. I made the title style work for the rest of the series and I really like the way they each turned out.

The hardest part about working on this book wasn't the book itself, but the fact that we bought our house just as I was finishing up the third draft. So the final stages of editing this book and designing the covers and doing the layout for this series was done in the midst of renovations to our new house. I was squeezing in time to work on this book just before going to work and even sometimes later at night just before I went to bed. I'm always writing!

I hope you enjoyed the book. If you did, please consider leaving a review on the retailer you bought it from or Goodreads. Not only do I read them all, but reviews help future readers decide if they'd like to buy a book, so even a simple review that says, "I liked it," helps!

– D. Allen
(JUNE 2018)

I'll be home for Christmas…

Tracy Slater may be a successful pop star, but fame and fortune isn't everything she thought it'd be. Under the thumb of a husband who is growing steadily more abusive, she's decided her marriage is over. She just needs to make it through one more trip home for the holidays with him before she's free.

If only in my dreams…

Stephen Austin worked hard to become the successful novelist he's always wanted to be. So why isn't he happy? And why does he feel so lonely? Then he runs into his old girlfriend, the one he thought he had lost forever.

Tormented by the mistakes of their past, Stephen sees his reunion with Tracy as a second chance. But does she feel the same way?

A Christmas Reunion

A Novella

—Small Town Christmas—
Book 1

❄ ❄ ❄

D. Allen

Chapter One
TRACY

DECEMBER 20TH

As my driver pulls into the airport, I worry that I made the wrong decision about coming home. There's just too much work to do. I'm not even going back to my place in LA since the press tour ended for the new album. I'm flying right from New York to Batavia. Charlie doesn't like it.

"Why don't I just go back to check in on things? I'll meet you back at your mom's place in a couple days," he pleaded last night.

"What am I supposed to tell Mom when I show up without my husband?" I retorted. Mom's always worried that I don't make enough time for family. She says I work too hard.

And now Charlie has refused to talk to me all day.

A Christmas Reunion

He stayed back at the hotel while I hit the gym this morning and met with my team at the label one last time before the holidays. He took the last few weeks off from work, claiming we'd be able to spend it together. Obviously he didn't pay attention the millions of times I told him that I had to work up until the third week of December.

What's really set him off is where the argument turned last night. Where it *always* turns: kids. He says he doesn't want to be in his sixties when our kids are just graduating high school.

The airport is crowded when Charlie and I enter. Typical of the holiday season, but before we even reach security, a group of girls stops us to get my autograph and take some pictures.

Charlie stands off to the side and flashes me his phone to show the time. No matter where I am I try to make time for anyone who approaches me for a picture. Charlie usually tells me to politely decline if I'm in a rush. He's not a fan of my career. He thinks that I should stop working at this "silly singing thing" and focus on being a mother.

Yeah, like he doesn't enjoy the private jet and the $3 million house this "silly singing thing" pays for. Not to mention his wardrobe of designer suits that he wears to impress his colleagues. I'm sure they know that I'm the

D. ALLEN

real moneymaker in our marriage. That's gotta be a blow to his fragile masculinity.

Just as the last of the girls is snapping a selfie of us on her phone, Charlie grabs my elbow and says, "Honey, we have a flight to catch."

After security we use a special exit that takes us onto the runway to board the private jet. It's equipped with the works—leather seats, kitchenette, TVs, you name it. It's practically a flying house.

"That was rude," I mutter as I take my seat.

"You're the one who is in such a rush to get home." He takes the seat behind me, which I don't question. We haven't really talked since last night's argument—not that we usually do—and emotions are still high.

Hopefully going to my mom's will alleviate some of the tension. Based on previous holidays and family gatherings, I know that as soon as we get to the front door, he'll turn on his charm and act like the proud, doting husband that he has everyone believing he is.

After I told my mom I was coming home for Christmas, she immediately told me about Daisy Doyle's grand idea to throw a holiday class reunion. I guess her married name is Daniels—still got those double Ds. Her husband has to be deaf. Or blind. Or both.

No, Daisy's not the worst person I've met. When you mingle with entitled celebrities and name-droppers,

A Christmas Reunion

your faith in humanity pretty much goes out the window. Daisy's just…intense sometimes. Or at least she was the last time I saw her ten years ago.

She wants me to sing something at the reunion. I don't even want to go. We'll see. It's supposed to be a pre-Christmas mixer to catch folks who are in town for the holidays. Everyone else probably already has plans for that day, so it's likely to be a dud. Maybe I can talk her out of having me sing.

It's not that I dislike singing. I love it. Obviously, I've made a career out of it. It's just that I've escalated into a different world than everyone else. "Show business." Singing will only shove my success in their faces and further prove that I'm different. That I no longer fit in with the rest of them.

Still, there are a few people I wouldn't mind catching up with. People I haven't seen since graduation. I had a lot of fun in high school. Besides my family, there isn't really anyone from back home that I still talk to, which is a shame.

I look out the window as the plane rises above the city. The lights beneath are beautiful. Mom would likely be trying to take a million pictures. Of course, she would have to ask for someone's help to find her camera app, then she'd complain about the glare from the window. I can't help but smile at that.

D. ALLEN

I'm anxious to see my mom. Since Dad died, her health has been slipping. Complications from her diabetes and congestive heart failure. My guess is she hasn't been watching her diet like she's supposed to. My sister, Kimmy, checks on her as often as she can, but she's married with two kids of her own. She's busy. I'm busy. So busy I can't even *call* my mother every week. I'm hoping this visit will help with some of that neglect.

The plane lands an hour or so later at the small county airport just outside the city. If you would've told me as a teenager that I'd be using it with my own private jet, I never would've believed you. But then, I never would've been able to predict any part of my adult life.

The brisk December wind hits me as Charlie and I descend the stairs onto the runway. My hair flies in my face and I don't notice my sister at first as she approaches, but I definitely hear her loud scream when she spots me.

A wide grin stretches across my face. Someone genuinely happy to see me for me, not just my accomplishments? I immediately feel at home. Besides, she's my big sister. Even though I'm extremely busy, I've managed to keep in touch with her through texts and the random tagging on Facebook.

"Oh, I've missed you so much!" she nearly shouts in my ear over the roar of the wind and the plane. She squeezes me as tight as she can in our puffy coats.

"I've missed you too!" I hold her out at arm's length. "You look so good! Did you cut your hair?"

Kimmy might as well be the antithesis of me. She has short-cropped brunette hair, I have long blonde hair—now platinum blonde due to my stylist determining I need a "bold" look. While she's always supported my career, she would never even think of pursuing the same profession. Too much detail on perfection, too much focus on beauty, too much exposure, too much time.

Besides, Kimmy's purpose in life has always been motherhood. Even before she had kids, she was always the more responsible one. The one to sacrifice her free time to make sure I got to class or practice on time. The one who treated our pets as her babies. Being a celebrity doesn't allow for time to start a family. Especially not when you're "Tracy Slater."

Kimmy reaches back and pats her bare neck. "Yeah. Do you think it's too much?"

"No!" I exclaim. "I think you should put a hat on in this weather, but it looks cute!"

My sister and husband exchange polite nods, but her attention returns to me.

Some of the airport staff usher us into the terminal, where Charlie finally speaks up. He goes in for an

D. ALLEN

awkward hug with Kimmy and says, "It's good to see you. You guys should come out to California sometime with the kids."

Yet another reason why we're not ready to have kids. Charlie just doesn't get it.

It's not like we don't have the room for my sister and her family. I would love to have her. It's just not feasible. Besides, what would the kids *do* at our house? Sure, we have the pool, but I just know Charlie will throw a fit when they start tracking the water inside the house or knocking too much of it out. And all of our "art"? Consider those gone, Chuckie.

My sister must sense my mood and politely smiles at my husband. "Maybe this summer we can meet up with you guys on tour. I know the boys loved it when Trace brought them on stage with the last one."

"Right. Yeah." The mention of my upcoming work obligations causes him to lose interest.

"Do we have everything?" I ask.

Normally my assistant would be on top of moving the schedule along—even if it's a vacation—but I gave her the rest of the year off. I already felt guilty for having her work so late into December. Usually I give her the whole month off, but the label wanted to push Black Friday and pre-Christmas sales, meaning press got bumped closer to the holidays.

A Christmas Reunion

"Yeah." Charlie grabs our bags and heads to the door to the parking lot.

Kimmy brings her eyebrows together and I roll my eyes in response.

❄ ❄ ❄

Nothing can quite compare to sitting in my childhood home decorated for Christmas with the fire crackling and the likes of Nat "King" Cole, Dean Martin, and Brenda Lee playing softly in the background. Add my mother's turkey casserole—likely made from leftover Thanksgiving fixings—and you have the perfect evening.

My sister couldn't stay for dinner. Her oldest son was in his first school play: *A Christmas Carol*. I guess he insisted that his parents go to all three showings. My mom went last night. Tonight is the final night, and I would've liked to go, but I didn't even bring it up. I knew Charlie would make a face and grumble the whole time. For someone who claims to want kids, he doesn't have a lot of tolerance for them.

Not to mention I still need to prepare myself to see everyone. Returning to my former high school in one of my camera-ready outfits is not what I want to do. I purposely packed jeans and modest sweaters to help blend in. I'm not here to upstage anyone.

"Has Daisy talked to you yet?" Mom asks as she pulls the casserole out of the oven.

I fuss with the corner of the forest-green placemat. "Sort of. I've e-mailed her a few times. She's mostly talked to Missy since I've been so busy with the album drop and everything."

"Missy?"

"My assistant."

"Oh." Mom nods. She begins dishing out our plates.

"Do you need any help, Mom?" Charlie asks. *Mom*? That's new.

She smiles. "No, dear, I've got it all under control. You two just take a seat."

Charlie sits back with a smug smile on his face.

When Mom joins us at the table, she continues, "You really should give Daisy a call. She's so happy you're back in town for a bit. She says everyone who's coming to the mixer is excited to see you."

"She told everyone I'm coming?" I groan.

"Well yeah, sweetie. They'll be happy to see you. Why are you upset?"

I shrug. "I don't know." I poke around my plate with my fork. It's not worth it to go into how people expect to see "Tracy Slater," the celebrity, when all I

A Christmas Reunion

want to be while I'm home is just Tracy, the old high school friend.

Charlie doesn't like it when I talk about the two sides of myself. Apparently it's bogus and I'm just fishing for attention. He doesn't get it. Not like he used to. When we first got together, I felt like he knew everything about me. Of course, we only dated while I was on tour and married shortly after it ended. I suppose it was like summer camp. It worked when we made a special effort to see each other, but now that we're married and have two very different careers, it's just not the same.

"I've got her number by the phone. Give her a call. Oh, not tonight, though. She's in charge of the school play."

I give a tight smile. "Of course she is."

"It's a shame we missed the play," Charlie says. He taps his plate with his fork. "This is very good. Thanks for making it."

I look down at my plate and roll my eyes. What an act.

"Oh, I'm glad you like it!" Mom smiles. "The play was cute. Maybe someday soon you two will be going for your kid."

"Mom!"

"That would be nice," Charlie adds.

"Tracy, you're not getting any younger. Trust me, I

D. ALLEN

was older when I had you girls, and there were certainly challenges. Look at me now! I may never get to see grandchildren from you."

"Don't say that!"

She shrugs. "I'm just saying…"

Charlie nods and looks at me.

I bite my lip and look away.

Mom gets up, grabs something from the counter, and hands it to me. It's one of the magazine covers I did. I haven't seen it yet, so it must've just come out.

"Tracy, I think it's great that you're doing so well, and you know how proud I am of you, but look at that. I'm just worried that you won't have any maternal instincts left if you keep things like this up."

I study the cover and try to determine what she's taken offense with. It's not one of my sultrier poses that she usually condemns. I'm actually smiling in this one!

"What is it?" I finally ask.

"Is there even a reason for you to be wearing a top if you're going to show off the girls anyway?" She shoves her hands under her breasts and gives a little shake. Not what I expected from a woman wearing a sweater with kittens in Santa hats.

My top in the picture is cut lower than I'm used to wearing, but it's still pretty modest compared to most magazine covers. Besides, compared to other pop stars,

A Christmas Reunion

I'm a saint. But based on the look on my mother's face, I look like a whore.

Charlie glances over. "Mmm, you're right. I don't know if I would've approved of that one if I were there."

I glare at him. First of all, he doesn't *approve* of anything I wear. Second, he *was* there, and I'm pretty sure he was drooling at some of the pictures that were taken. I believe he told me later that I don't fix myself up for him like I do for the camera. And yet, he's stumped why we don't have more sex.

I toss the magazine back on the table. "Mom, these covers are all digitally modified."

"And you're okay with that? What if they changed it so you were naked on the cover?"

"Well, they can't do *that*."

"Then why didn't you ask to see the final photos?"

"If I asked to see the final photos for every picture that's taken of me, I'd never get anything else done!"

"I agree with your mother," Charlie cuts in. "You need to be careful about what you're putting out for the world to see. Our future kids will be seeing things like this eventually."

Mom nods.

"Charlie…" I growl between my teeth.

He knows. He knows exactly what circumstances I'm in. He knows how busy I am and how carefully I put together my brand. Showing some cleavage doesn't ruin that. I know what I'm doing. I've been doing it for years. Besides, my children—if I decide to have them—will know how to respect women.

But if he agrees with me, he can't play up to my mother's expectations of being the perfect son-in-law. I know she sees through the ruse sometimes, but other times I can't believe how gullible she is.

My mother's objections to some of my career choices don't bother me. She usually nitpicks the little things, but I know she's proud of the big things. It seems like she takes an ad out in the paper every time I win an award. And to my knowledge, she's never missed one of my performances on TV—thanks to Kimmy showing her how to use the DVR. She's definitely always been cheering me on, even if she has an opinion on some things.

What bothers me is my husband's complete abandonment of support whenever it suits him. Sometimes I wish he would just go away.

My old bedroom is now a guest room. The flowery wallpaper remains, as well as the spot by the closet door that I had used as a coloring canvas when I was six. I remember my mother scrubbing at it for a long time, working away the colorful wax. It still stained the paper, leaving an odd salmon color.

It's a small room for a double bed, but without any other furniture besides a dresser and an end table, it works. What I'm not looking forward to is sharing such a tight space with Charlie. At home we have a king size, so I can pretty much put as much space between us as I need. Besides, our work schedules differ so much we barely spend any time together in the same bed.

"You seemed awfully chummy with my mom," I say as I unload my clothes into the dresser.

"And you seemed awfully pissy." He lies against the headboard, his eyes on his phone.

"At least I'm not putting on a show for everyone."

"It's what you do every day. You should be used to it. What did you tell me? There are two versions of you? Which version am I getting now?"

I slam the dresser shut. "Never mind. You obviously don't get it." I try to walk by him and out the door, but he grabs ahold of my arm.

"Hey, come here." He stands and pulls me into a hug. He has my arms pinned to my side, making it impossible to return it. "Just try to lighten up. It is the holidays, after all."

He leans in for a kiss, but I back away.

D. ALLEN

"Lighten up? I'm not the one ruining everyone's time."

"Really? You're ruining my time."

"Maybe that's your problem, then."

He overturns his hands. "I think you're the one with the problem. What's the matter? You've been short with me ever since we got here. Before that, even."

I cross my arms and glare at him. "Do you really want to do this now?"

"If it's the only time I can get you to open up, then yes. Let's do this now."

I study him, trying to decipher whether he knows what I'm thinking. This relationship has turned hostile in the last year. I've lost an unhealthy amount of weight. His anger has been growing steadily, not to mention his back acne. Add the cost of his dermatologist and expensive zit cream to the tab of his sugar mama.

"This isn't working anymore."

He looks confused. Clearly we're not on the same page. Either that or he's playing dumb to make me look like the bitch. Wouldn't be the first time.

"What are you talking about?" he asks.

"I want a divorce."

"What?"

I shrug. "Or a separation or something. Maybe see a counselor until we figure it out. But for the time being, you and I can't solve our problems on our own."

He shakes his head. "No, we're not separating. I'm not divorcing you."

"Okay, so *I'll* divorce *you*. If I want to end the marriage, there's really nothing you can do about it." That last bit of information came straight from an attorney I've already got on retainer.

"No."

I squint my eyes at him. "No?"

"Little Miss Tracy Slater is going to get over herself and actually think about someone else for a change. It's time you showed me a little respect."

"Respect?" I fight to keep my voice down. "Charlie, you constantly discredit my accomplishments."

He rolls his eyes. "Please, you're not curing cancer."

"And you are?" He's an investment banker. Basically, shifting money around. Back when I met him, he was my reminder than real people have day jobs. That, and the label loved that his company was always willing to sponsor my shows.

"That's enough. Now let's put on a happy smile and go enjoy the holidays with your mother, which you insisted on."

"I never get to see her, Charlie!" I whisper-shout. "None of my family. I think I deserve to spend a week with them for Christmas."

"And what about my family? You don't think I want to see them?"

"We just saw them for Thanksgiving! Not to mention the cruise we went on last summer with your brother, or don't you remember the private yacht you insisted I pay half for?"

"*We* paid half for!"

"That's funny, because I'm pretty sure the cash came out of *my* account."

"*Our* account."

"You can say that all you want, but I still make more than you, and that's a fact you can't stand."

I'm thrown onto the small bed, his finger in my face.

"Just because you sell yourself out like a cheap whore doesn't mean you can throw it in my face!"

I stare at him, my heart pounding in my chest.

He balls his fist near my face. "And you keep your mouth shut about this divorce business."

I watch as he leaves, still frozen in place. My heart races. I hate that man. I want him gone. But in this tiny bedroom and with the approaching holiday, I'm trapped.

Chapter Two
STEPHEN
DECEMBER 20TH

I find myself at the bar on Jackson Street again tonight. The muse just isn't with me. Hasn't been in a while. Sometimes I wonder if the height of my career—and my life—is behind me. The magic lost.

Three bestselling books and several other critically acclaimed and fan-favorite books have graced my writing career, but the well has run dry. My publisher pesters me every week for something new. I haven't put out a new book in almost two years. Haven't written anything decent in just about six months.

Of course, it doesn't help that whenever I hear from my editor, she's always saying things like, "Can't wait to read what you've cooked up next!" or "If your previous books are any indication, we're all in for a real treat!"

Despite not writing a single thing today, my shoulders are knotted with stress. I need to unwind. The weight of failure sits heavy on me, making it even harder to finally write the story I intend to.

The bartender is new. His plain white T-shirt almost seems to bring out the baby fat he still has on his cheeks. Despite his recent employment, I've been coming here so frequently lately that he doesn't have to ask what I want. The bottle's at my usual spot before I even sit down.

"Thanks," I say before I take my first sip.

He wipes the bar with a rag. "You went to school here in town, right?"

I nod.

He pulls a flyer from the wall behind the bar and sets it beside me. "This your class?"

It's an announcement for my ten-year class reunion. The preholiday "mixer" is here. They rent out the restaurant part of the bar now and then for private events.

I've seen the flyers. I got the e-mails.

"Yeah, that's me."

"You going?"

I shake my head. "Probably not."

A Christmas Reunion

He shrugs. "Could be fun. Compare how well you're doing to how your former classmates are."

I roll my eyes. "I didn't like them in high school. I'm not going to like them now." I push the flyer away. "Remind me to stay away that night."

He pins it back on the wall and lets me have my space for a while. I read the news headlines on the TV above the liquor display.

"Hank tells me you're a writer."

I snort in response. "Sort of."

"Have you written anything recently?"

I shake my head now and sip my drink.

"Writer's block?"

I nod. "More like loss of talent."

He busies himself with dusting the liquor bottles on the shelves behind him. It's a Wednesday. A slow night.

"I wouldn't go that far," he says. "You'll figure something out."

I brush him off. He doesn't know the story. He doesn't know me. He's still young and naïve. Thinks everything will work out in the end. Well I've been to the end. I know that life doesn't always have a happily ever after. Not like the ones I'm known for writing.

It's funny, but if my readers actually knew who the real G.W. Austin was, they likely wouldn't buy my books. Not just because I'm a man, but because I'm a talentless drunk. Nothing like the swoon-worthy men I write about. God, sometimes I hate myself. I'm a sellout.

"What kind of books do you write, anyway?" the newbie asks. If Hank were here, he'd know to leave me the hell alone by now.

I give him the benefit of the doubt and decide to humor him. "Funnily enough, romance. I started out writing mysteries. The ones with the heavy romance backstories took off. My editor said I had a knack for writing about people in love. Once I wrote a straight-up romance, the publisher didn't want anything else from me." I shrug. "It sells."

"So what's the problem, then?"

"There's nothing left."

He can't be much older than twenty-one, twenty-two at most. A kid. He scrunches his face in confusion.

"I'm not writing," I add. "The inspiration is gone. Whatever I come up with sucks. New York's never gonna buy that. The characters are forced, the vocabulary is juvenile. I just can't write a believable romance anymore. Starting from scratch with a new genre will result in my reputation being destroyed. Poof! Gone."

My words are crueler than I intend, but the kid doesn't seem to take offense. Working in a bar will do that to you, I guess.

A Christmas Reunion

He places the bottle of whiskey he finished dusting back on the shelf. "You ever been in love yourself? Maybe that's the problem."

I finish off my drink. "Have I ever been in love? Sure. Once." I pull a ten out of my wallet and set it on the bar. This wasn't as relaxing as I thought it'd be. I'm not about to talk about my feelings to the local barkeep. This isn't a fucking romance novel. Then again, a scene like that would probably end up in the crap I've come up with lately. "That was a long time ago, kid. I'll see you around."

The brisk cold air hits me when I walk outside. Burying my hands in my pockets, I set off for the walk back to my house. It's not far. Maybe ten minutes. As I turn the corner onto Main Street, I nearly collide with two women.

"Oh, I'm sorr—Tracy?"

"Steve?" Her face lights up, and she takes me in for a moment before she reaches up for a hug. "How are you?" she says into my shoulder.

I quickly pat her back and pull away. Returning my hands to my pockets, I say, "Good. I didn't know you were home. It's, uh—"

She nods. "Yeah, it's…" There's a smile on her face, but she doesn't seem to know where to look.

Neither do I. Our footprints in the snow and the

ice collecting on the edge of the street suddenly have my interest.

This is Tracy. My Tracy. Right in front of me. "It's good to see you."

"Yeah, I just got in tonight. I'm —"

"You staying with your sister?" I interrupt. "Sorry, you go."

She smiles and looks down. "No."

"My house is too crazy with the kids," Kimmy adds. I've almost forgotten she's there.

"Right."

"You still live here in town?" Tracy asks.

As hard as I try, I can't keep the smile from my face. "Yup. Over on Summit."

She nods. "Gotcha. I'm staying with my mother for the holidays. We should catch up sometime before I leave. Maybe get some coffee or something?"

"Yeah, I'd like that." I hold her gaze for a while. I divert my eyes to the ground and kick the snow off my sneakers on the sidewalk. "Well, I've gotta get going."

"Right. Me too. We're going to grab something to eat. It was good seeing you."

"You too." I look to her sister. "Nice to see you again, Kimmy."

"Steve," she says with a nod.

During my walk home I'm numb for reasons

completely unrelated to the weather. That was the one and only Tracy Slater. The source of all the emotion I put into my books—or used to. The love of my life in high school. The girl I tried my hardest to get over. For a while I thought I had. And then she began popping up on TV and the radio, and I couldn't escape her or the perfect life she'd created for herself.

But still, I know I'll have a hard time getting her out of my head. She was my world. Things like that don't just go away. Especially when I have nothing to show for my life. No wife, no girlfriend, no kids. Just me.

I have no intention of catching up with her. It wouldn't do me any good. She's moved on. She's married. She has a life out in California. I'm just a memory to her.

Chapter Three
TRACY

DECEMBER 21ST

I'm sitting outside the Tim Horton's on Main Street. I have to talk myself up before I can go inside. Suddenly the apps on my phone require immediate, thorough attention. The low murmur of Christmas music coming from the speakers is the only thing that fills the air.

Daisy wanted to see me "right away" to discuss the possibility of me singing at the mixer. I'm only here to talk her out of it. Well, that's not the only reason. I needed to get out of the house. Mom went to pick up some last-minute gifts, so it was just me and Charlie. At the moment, Daisy is the lesser of two evils.

With a deep breath, I put on my big girl pants and step out into the cold. Inside, Daisy has already claimed a table. She calls my name from across the small café when she sees me and waves her hand in the air. She's wearing a red sweater and jeans. From what I can tell, she's kept in shape. But then, it's only our ten-year reunion. For the most part, everyone still has their youth. Just look at me and how much I'm exploiting it.

I wait in line to grab a cup of tea and head over to Daisy's table. She hugs me like we're old friends, not keeping her voice down at all. Announcing to the world that she's chummy with "Tracy Slater."

It's funny, because the people in the café likely wouldn't believe I am who I am just by looking at me. Or they just plain don't care. I'm not in my stage clothes. I'm not dressed for a photo shoot. I'm dressed for a trip to the coffee shop. In my black peacoat with my hair pulled back, I'm a normal person. That's part of the reason why I needed this trip. To get back in touch with reality.

"Oh my God, so how have you been?" She bends like a pretzel in her seat, legs crossed, leaning on her palm, eyes wide, and ready for any pop star story I might have for her.

"I'm doing okay." I'm not about to name-drop. "Just released the new record, so up until I got in last night, I haven't really had a chance to unwind from the press tour and everything else. I'm ready to just relax."

"I know! You've been all over the place, girl. I *love*

the new album. 'Bittersweet Memories' is probably my favorite. And it's great because I can listen to your stuff with the kids in the car." She puts her hand in front of me on the table and sits back. "Oh my God! You *have* to sign something for my niece! I would be *the* best aunt ever! Mine are still too young, but Abby *loves* you!"

I take a sip of my tea. I should've gotten coffee. Black. Better yet, vodka.

"How old is she?"

"Thirteen. You are her favorite. She doesn't believe me when I tell her we were friends in high school."

"Thirteen." I groan. "You couldn't pay me enough to go back to thirteen."

"Ugh, I know! But it's not like you have money trouble." She laughs loudly.

"Luckily, that's all behind us." I sidestep the money comment. "I know a lot of people probably don't even want to come to this reunion because of all the bad memories." If my media training taught me anything, it was how to steer a conversation back to the point of the meeting.

"Right? That's, like, what I'm afraid of. That nobody will show." Another exaggerated groan. "But I've got flyers *everywhere*. People will come. It's just one night! It's not like we have to relive high school all over again! Wouldn't that be the worst? Ugh!" She giggles loudly, and for just a minute, I feel like I really am back in high school.

"Yeah, I'm sure people will come. I'll be there." Guess that decides that, then. "Even if it's only a few people, it'll be more of an intimate gathering than a big party. The real reunion isn't until this summer, right?"

"Oh yeah! I want to do a couple get-togethers. You know, just to try to coincide with everyone's busy schedules. If you can't make it to one, you can make it to the other. Do you think you'll be coming this summer?"

I grit my teeth. "Oh, I don't know. I'll probably be in the middle of tour. We're still finalizing dates. It really depends on if I have a show and where I am."

"Well that's a bummer." She pulls out a folder and spreads it flat on the table. Slipping a piece of paper from one of the pockets, she pulls out a pen and says, "That's why you need to sing something for this mixer. Give everyone from high school a run for their money, huh?" She laughs in almost that Janice from *Friends* laugh, and I swear it's worse than when I get the high-pitched feedback in my in-ears on tour.

"Yeah, I actually wanted to talk to you about that…"

She doesn't hear me. "So I was thinking we could do a mix at the mixer." Another laugh. God help me. People are staring now, and it has nothing to do with my fame. "I've heard your Christmas EP and it was, *ugh*, beautiful! You have to sing a few things from that! But then I was thinking that people might be getting sick of Christmas songs by now, so you'll need to sing some of your other hits, too. 'Someday' or 'When Will You Be Mine?' or something like that. The big ones, you know?"

"Daisy, I don't really feel comfortable singing at the event."

Her face drops. "Why not?"

"Well, for one, I don't even have my band with me or any of the other equipment we'd need."

She waves a limp hand at me. "That's okay. Maybe just a few a cappella numbers. You could do 'Silent Night' or 'Have Yourself a Merry Little Christmas.' People love those. They're classics. Besides, you've got the voice for it. Of course, we'll have to narrow it down a bit. One or two—"

"That's not…singing is what I do for a living. It's work. I love it, but when I'm meeting up with old friends, I don't want to have to worry about all that. I'm sorry. I'll help in any other way I can, but I don't want to sing."

Daisy lets out an exaggerated breath of air. "Okay. I suppose that's fair. You *are* on vacation, after all. I forget that this isn't home for you anymore."

That hits me harder than I expect it to. This will always be home. But have I been treating it like that?

Not really. I've neglected this town and the people in it since I first saw success. Maybe, against all my efforts not to, I've become a diva so far separated from reality that I can't even identify what really matters anymore.

She closes her folder and sits back, cradling her drink. "Well, I pretty much have everything else figured out. You could come early and help set up, but I mostly wanted to talk to you about what you were going to sing."

I cringe. "Sorry."

Another limp wrist wave. "Don't worry about it. It's okay. It's not like I announced it. I just thought it'd be a nice surprise."

Shrugging, I admit, "Yeah, it would've been."

"Who are you most anxious to see?"

"Me? I don't know." I'm not positive what she implies by "anxious." "Everyone, I guess. I don't really talk to people from high school anymore, so it'll be nice to see everyone."

Daisy rolls her eyes. "Stop being polite! Come on, just between girlfriends, who is it?"

I stutter, not coming up with a coherent answer. And side note—girlfriends? Really?

"Okay, so who are you hoping doesn't come? Or comes but clearly still doesn't have their stuff together, know what I'm saying?" She covers her smirk when she

D. ALLEN

takes a sip of her drink.

I can't help but laugh with her. Despite how annoying she can be, Daisy was always nice to me. I guess I don't mind her company now and then. In moderation. At the moment, I'm content with our chitchatting. It makes me feel normal. Enough that I let myself indulge in a little gossip.

"Is Christie Harowski still around?"

Daisy's eyes light up. "Oh my God! You didn't hear?"

"No, what happened to her?"

"Okay, so after high school, you know how Christie had gotten accepted to Cornell and was going on and on about how she was going to get her master's degree and blah blah blah? Well, that never happened. She went, but during the first semester she got pregnant by some frat boy. She came back here to have the baby and got a job at Walmart. Okay fine. She was working, providing for the baby. Cool. But then, *apparently*, she got in with this one guy who…let's just say he ran a side business out of his car—"

"Really?" I'm leaning in on the table.

She holds up her hand. "That's what I heard. One way or another, she ended up hooked on God-only-knows what, let the baby cry while she was hyped up on whatever she took. A neighbor heard and called CPS.

The baby went into foster care and she has to have supervised visits."

My mind has officially been blown. She was in the top ten of our class! She had almost a full ride to Cornell! Last time I heard about her, her life was set.

"Damn." I can't hide my smile. It's horrible to get satisfaction off of someone else's misfortune, but she was not a nice person in high school. Karma is real.

"Yup. So even if she does show up, you have nothing to worry about. Actually, you have nothing to worry about with anyone. You're, hands down, *the* most successful person from our class."

I sip my drink, my mood soured a bit. "I don't know if that's true." The conversation has once again slipped back to my lifestyle. Maybe I need to rethink even going to the reunion.

"Tracy, are you kidding me right now? You have — what? — three multiplatinum records, a fourth on the way, and have made millions traveling the world and being this awesome businesswoman. I think you're pretty successful."

"There's more to success than just a career." I turn my attention to the window, watching as the cars navigate the drive-thru in the wet snow that has been smushed to slush.

"Well, you're married, right?"

D. ALLEN

I nod. "Yeah."

She slaps the table and my eyes jerk back to her, nearly spilling my tea all over myself.

"Oh my God! I just got the *best* idea! We should have everyone bring in old pictures for a photo collage! Yeah, we could get everyone's school photos from the yearbooks throughout the years! Ah! It'll be *so cute*!"

I grin. "Not sure how happy some people will be about that, but yeah, it's a great idea." I know I made some horrible fashion choices back in the day. That's why I have a stylist now.

"Maybe some candids, too. That'd be fun. Gosh, there's probably *so many* pictures of you and Steve Austin. You still talk to him?"

Tucking my hair behind my ear, I say, "Uh, not really. I ran into him last night. Quite literally, actually."

"Shut up! Oh, my heart is breaking! Everyone thought you two would get married!"

"Well, I am married. To someone else. Not Steve." I'm not sure if I'm trying to remind Daisy or myself. "And besides, he's probably got a girlfriend or a wife or something too."

Daisy shakes her head. "I don't think so, Trace. Ugh, you two were *so cute*! What happened?"

I finish off my tea. "Um…just grew apart, I guess. Listen, I've gotta run. It was nice seeing you." I pull on

A Christmas Reunion

my coat and give her a wave before heading out the door.

Stephen. If he's single, it makes me wonder what he's been up to for the last ten years. Personally, that is. From what I've seen, he's built a good career for himself. But I can't see him. Not on this trip. Not with everything going on with Charlie. Charlie would get the wrong idea about me wanting a divorce. He'd go to the papers, leak some fictional story.

No. My best option is to stay as far away from Stephen Austin as I possibly can.

More by the Author

To find more books by the author, visit
DavidNethBooks.com/Books

* * *

Subscribe to his newsletter to be the first to know of new
releases and special deals!
DavidNethBooks.com/Newsletter

* * *

If you enjoyed the book, please consider leaving a review
on Goodreads or the retailer you bought it from. Reviews
help potential readers determine whether they'll enjoy a
book, so any comments on what you thought of the story
would be very helpful!

About the Author

D. Allen is the author of the sweet small town romance series, Montana Beach and Small Town Christmas.

Also writes fantasy and superhero fiction as David Neth.

www.DavidNethBooks.com
www.facebook.com/DavidNethBooks

www.ingramcontent.com/pod-product-compliance
Lightning Source LLC
Chambersburg PA
CBHW021549310726
48972CB00003B/742